"Me?"

The startled squeak of Sheryl's voice echoed off the walls of the little-used office.

"You," Harry confirmed, pulling a folded document out of his coat pocket. "This authorizes an indefinite detail. You're on my team, effective immediately."

"Hey, hang on here," Sheryl protested. "I'm not sure I want to be assigned to a fugitive apprehension task force, indefinitely or otherwise. Before I agree to anything like this, I want to know what's required of me."

"Basically, I want your exclusive time and attention for as long as it takes to extract every bit of information I can."

Sheryl stared at him. "Exclusive time and attention? You mean, like all day?"

Harry forced his expression to stay neutral as he answered, "And all night, if necessary."

SAFE HAVEN

MERLINE LOVELACE

Return to Sender

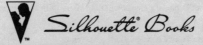

Published by Silhouette Books
America's Publisher of Contemporary Romance

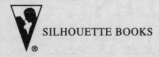

SILHOUETTE BOOKS

ISBN-13: 978-0-373-36190-8
ISBN-10:   0-373-36190-4

RETURN TO SENDER

Copyright © 1998 by Merline Lovelace

Printed in U.S.A.

MERLINE LOVELACE

launched a second career as a writer after twenty-three years commanding U.S. Forces around the world. She bases many of her tales on her own experiences in uniform and on her travels to the four corners of the globe. This *USA TODAY* bestselling author has now published more than sixty-five novels, and her books have won numerous awards, including the Romance Writers of America's prestigious RITA®. Readers can find out more about Merline at her Web site, www.merlinelovelace.com.

This one's for Sherrill and Elisha and Peggy and all the folks at the S. Penn Post Office—thanks for your friendly smiles when I show up all drawn and haggard to put a finished manuscript in the mail. Thanks, too, for your cheerful professionalism. You're outstanding representatives of the finest postal system in the world!

Chapter 1

Rio de Janeiro.

Mount Sugarloaf rising majestically above the city.

Streets crowded with revelers in costumes of bright greens and yellows and reds.

The glossy postcard leaped out at Sheryl Hancock from the thick sheaf of mail. Her hand stilled its task of sorting and stuffing post office boxes. The familiar early-morning sounds of co-workers grumbling and letters whooshing into metal boxes faded. For the briefest moment, she caught a faint calypso beat in the rattle of a passing mail cart and heard the laughter of Carnival.

"Is that another postcard from Paul-boy?"

With a small jolt, Sheryl left the South America festival and returned to the Albuquerque post office where she'd worked for the past twelve years. Smiling at the woman standing a few feet away, she nodded.

"Yes. This one's from Rio."

"Rio? The guy sure gets around, doesn't he?"

Elise Hart eased her bulk around a bank of opened postal boxes to peer at the postcard in Sheryl's hand. From the expression in Elise's brown eyes, it was obvious that she, too, was feeling the momentary magic of faraway places.

"What does this one say?"

Sheryl flipped the card over. "'Hi to my favorite aunt. I've been dancing in the streets for the past four days. Wish you were here.'"

Sighing, Elise gazed at the slick card. "What I wouldn't give to dump my two boys with my mother and fly down to Rio for Carnival."

"Oh, sure. I can just see you dancing through the streets, eight months pregnant yet."

"Eight months, one week, two days and counting," the redhead replied with a grimace. "I'd put on my dancing shoes for a hunk like Mrs. Gunderson's nephew, though."

"You'd better not put on dancing shoes! I'm your birthing partner, remember? I don't want you going into premature labor on me. Besides," Sheryl tacked on, "we only have Mrs. Gunderson's word for it that her nephew qualifies as a hunk."

"According to his doting aunt, Paul-boy sports a thick mustache, specializes in tight jeans and rates about 112 on the gorgeous scale." Elise waggled her dark-red brows in an exaggerated leer. "That's qualification enough in my book."

"Paul-boy, as you insist on calling him, is also pushing forty."

"So?"

So Sheryl didn't have a whole lot of respect for jet-setting playboys who refused to grow up or grow into their responsibilities. Her father had been a pharmaceutical salesman by profession and a wanderer by nature. He'd drifted in and out of her life for short periods during her youth, until her mother's loneliness and bitter nagging had made him disappear altogether. Sheryl didn't blame him, exactly. More often than not, she herself had to grit her teeth when her mother called in one of her complaining moods. But neither did she like to talk about her absent parent.

Instead, she teased Elise about her fascination with the man they both heard about every time the frail, white-haired woman who'd moved to Albuquerque some four months ago came in to collect her mail.

"Don't you think Mrs. Gunderson might be just a bit prejudiced about this nephew of hers?"

"Maybe. He still sounds yummy." Sighing, Elise rested a hand on her high, rounded stomach. "You'd think I would have learned my lesson once and for all. My ex broke the gorgeous scale, too."

Sheryl had bitten down hard on her lip too many times in the past to keep from criticizing her friend's husband. Since their divorce seven months ago, she felt no such restraints.

"Rick also weighed in as a total loser."

"True," Elise agreed. "He was, is and always will be

a jerk." She traced a few absent circles on her tummy. "We can't all find men like Brian, Sher."

At the mention of her almost-fiancé, Sheryl banished any lingering thoughts of Elise's ex, Latin American carnivals and the globe-trotting Paul Gunderson. In their place came the easy slide of contentment that always accompanied any thought of Brian Mitchell.

"No, we can't," she confirmed.

"So have you two set a date yet?"

"We're talking about an engagement at the end of the year."

"You're engaged to get engaged." Her friend's brown eyes twinkled. "That's so…so Brian."

"I know."

Actually, the measured pace of Sheryl's relationship with the Albuquerque real estate agent satisfied her almost as much as it did him. After dating for nearly a year, they'd just started talking about the next step. They'd announce an engagement when the time was right, quite possibly at Christmas, and set a firm date for the wedding when they'd saved up enough to purchase a house. Brian was sure interest rates would drop another few points in the next year or so. Before they took the plunge into matrimony, he wanted to be in a position to buy down their monthly house payments so they could live comfortably on her salary and his commissions.

"I think that's what I like most about him," Sheryl confided. "His dependability and careful planning and—"

"Not to mention his cute buns."

"Well…"

"Ha! Don't give me that Little Miss Innocent look. I know you, girl. Under that sunshine-and-summer exterior, you crave excitement and passion as much as the next woman. Even fat, prego ones."

"What I crave," Sheryl replied, laughing, "is for you to get back to work. We've only got ten minutes until opening, and I don't want to face the hordes lined up in the lobby by myself."

Elise made a face and dipped into the cardboard tray in front of her for another stack of letters. She and Sheryl had come in early to help throw the postal box mail, since the clerk who regularly handled it was on vacation. They'd have to scramble to finish the last wall of boxes and get their cash drawers out of the vault in time to man the front counter.

Swiftly, Sheryl shuffled through the stack in her hand for the rest of Mrs. Gunderson's mail. Today's batch was mostly junk, she saw. Coupon booklets. Advertising fliers. A preprinted solicitation from the state insurance commissioner facing a special runoff election next week. And the postcard from Paul-boy, as Elise had dubbed him. With a last, fleeting glance at the colorful street scene, Sheryl bent down to stuff the mail into Mrs. Gunderson's slot.

It wouldn't stuff.

Frowning, she dropped down on her sneakered heels to examine the three-by-five-inch box. It contained at least one, maybe two days' worth of mail.

Strange. Mrs. Gunderson usually came into the post office every day to pick up her mail. More often than not, she'd pop in to chat with the employees on the counter, her yappy black-and-white shih tzu tucked under her arm. Regulations prohibited live animals in the post office except for those being shipped, but no one had the heart to tell Inga Gunderson that she couldn't bring her baby inside with her. Particularly when she also brought in homemade cookies and melt-in-your-mouth Danish spice cakes.

A niggle of worry worked into Sheryl's mind as she shoved Mrs. Gunderson's mail into her box. She hoped the woman wasn't sick or incapacitated. She'd keep an eye out for her today, just to relieve her mind that she was okay. Pushing off her heels, she finished the wall of boxes with brisk efficiency and headed for the vault. She had less than five minutes to count out her cash drawer and restock her supplies.

She managed it in four. She was at the front counter, her ready smile in place, when the branch manager unlocked the glass doors to the lobby and the first of the day's customers streamed in.

Sheryl didn't catch a glimpse of Mrs. Gunderson all morning, nor did any of her co-workers. As the day wore on, the unclaimed mail nagged at Sheryl. During her lunch break, she checked the postal box registry for the elderly renter's address and phone number.

The section of town where Inga Gunderson lived was served by another postal station much closer to her house, Sheryl noted. Wondering why the woman would choose to rent a box at a post office so far from her home, she dialed the number. The phone rang twice, then clicked to an answering machine. Since leaving a message wouldn't do anything to assure her of the woman's well-being, Sheryl hung up in the middle of the standard I-can't-come-to-the-phone-right-now recording.

Having come in at six-thirty to help "wall" the letters for the postal boxes, she got off at three. A quick check of Mrs. Gunderson's box showed it was still stuffed with unclaimed mail. Frowning, Sheryl wove her way slowly through the maze of route carriers' work areas and headed for the women's locker room at the rear of the station. After peeling off her pin-striped uniform shirt, she replaced it with a yellow tank top that brightened up the navy shorts worn by most of the postal employees in summer. A glance at the clock on the wall had her grabbing for her purse. She'd promised to meet Brian at three-thirty to look at a property he was thinking of listing.

After extracting a promise from Elise to go right home and get off her feet, Sheryl stepped outside. Hot, dry heat hit her like a slap in the face. With the sun beating down on her head and shoulders, she crossed the asphalt parking lot toward her trusty, ice-blue Camry. She opened the door and waited a moment to let the captured heat pour out. As she stood there in the hot, blazing sun, her nagging worry over Mrs. Gunderson crystallized into real concern. She'd swing by the woman's house, she decided. Just to check on her. It was a little out of her way, but Sheryl couldn't shake the fear that something had happened to the frail, white-haired customer.

With the Toyota's air conditioner doing valiant battle

against the heat, she pulled out of the parking lot behind the post office and headed west on Haines, then north on Juan Tabo. Two more turns and three miles took her to the shady, residential neighborhood and Inga Gunderson's neat, two-story adobe house. She didn't see a car in the driveway, although several were parked along the street. Maybe Mrs. Gunderson's car was in the detached rear garage. Or maybe she'd gone out of town. Or maybe…

Maybe she was ill, or had fallen down the stairs and broken a leg or a hip. The woman lived alone, with only her precious Button for company. She could be lying in the house now, helpless and in pain.

More worried than ever, Sheryl pulled into the driveway and climbed out of the car. Once more the heat enveloped her. She could almost feel her hair sizzling. The thick, naturally curly mane tended to turn unmanageable at the best of times. In this soul-sucking heat, it took on a life of its own. Tucking a few wildly corkscrewing strands into the loose French braid that hung halfway down her back, Sheryl followed a pebbled walk to the front porch. A feathery Russian olive tree crowded the railed porch and provided welcome shade. Sighing in relief, she pressed the doorbell.

When the distant sound of a buzzer produced a series of high, plaintive yips and no Mrs. Gunderson, Sheryl's concern vaulted into genuine alarm. Inga Gunderson wouldn't leave town without her Button. The two were practically joined at the hip. They even looked alike, Elise had once joked, both possessing slightly pug noses, round, inquisitive eyes and hair more white than black.

Sheryl leaned on the doorbell again, and heard a

chorus of even more frantic yaps. She pulled open the screen and pounded on the door.

"Mrs. Gunderson! Are you in there?"

A long, piteous yowl answered her call. She hammered on the door in earnest, setting the frosted-glass panes to rattling.

"Mrs. Gunderson! Are you okay?"

Button howled once more, and Sheryl reached for the old fashioned iron latch. She had just closed her hand around it when the door snapped open, jerking her inside with it.

Gasping, she found herself nose to nose with a wrinkled linen sport coat and a blue cotton shirt that stretched across a broad chest. A *very* broad chest. She took a quick step back, at which point several things happened at once, none of them good from her perspective.

Her foot caught on the door mat, throwing her off balance.

A hard hand shot out and grabbed her arm, either to save her from falling or to prevent her escape.

A tiny black-and-white fury erupted from inside the house. Gums lifted, needle-sharp teeth bared, it flew through the air and fastened its jaws on the jean-clad calf of her rescuer-captor.

"Ow!"

The man danced across the porch on one booted foot, taking Sheryl with him. Cursing, he lifted his leg and shook it. The little shih tzu snarled ferociously and hung on with all the determination of the rat catcher he was originally bred to be. Snarling a little herself, Sheryl tried to shake free of the bruising hold on her arm. When the stranger didn't loosen his grip, she dug her nails into the back of his tanned hand.

"Dammit, let go!"

She didn't know if the command shouted just above her ear was directed at her or the dog, and didn't particularly care. Pure, undiluted adrenaline pumped through her veins. She had no idea who this man was or what had happened to Mrs. Gunderson, but obviously *something* had. Something Button didn't like. Sheryl's only thought was to get away, find a phone, call the police.

Her attacker gave his upraised leg another shake, and Sheryl gouged her nails deeper into his skin. When that earned her a smothered curse and a painful jerk on her arm, she took a cue from the shih tzu and bent to bite the hand that held her.

"Hey!"

Still half-bent, Sheryl felt herself spun sideways. Her captor released his grip, but before she could bolt, his arm whipped around her waist. A half second later, she thudded back into the solid wall of blue oxford.

Her breath slammed out of her lungs. The band around her middle cut off any possibility of pulling in a replacement supply. As frantic now as the dog, she kicked back. One sneakered heel connected with the man's shin.

"Oh, for…!" Lifting her off her feet, her attacker grunted in her ear. "Calm down! I won't hurt you."

"Prove…it." she panted. "Let…me…go!"

"I will, I will. Just calm down."

Sheryl calmed, for the simple reason that she couldn't do anything else. Her ribs felt as though they'd threaded right through one another and squeezed out everything in between. Red spots danced before her eyes.

Thankfully, the excruciating pressure on her waist eased. She drew great gulps of air into her starved lungs. The sounds of another snarl and another curse battered at her ears. They were followed by a wheezy whine. When the spots in front of her eyes cleared, she turned to face a belligerent male, holding an equally belligerent shih tzu by the scruff of its neck.

For the first time, she saw the man's face. It was as hard as the rest of his long, lean body, Sheryl decided shakily. The sun had weathered his skin to dark oak. White lines fanned the corners of his eyes. They showed whiskey gold behind lashes the same dark brown as his short, straight hair and luxuriant mustache.

His mustache!

Sheryl whipped her gaze down his rangy form. Beneath the blue cotton shirt and tan jacket, his jeans molded trim hips and tight, corded thighs. She made the connection with a rush of relief.

The hunky nephew!

She'd have to tell Elise that Mrs. Gunderson wasn't all that far-off in her description. Although Sheryl wouldn't quite rate this rugged, whipcord-lean man as 112 on the gorgeous scale, he definitely scored at least an 88 or 90. Well, maybe a 99.

Wedging the yapping shih tzu under his arm like a hairy football, he gave Sheryl a narrow-eyed once-over. "Sorry about the little dance we just did. Are you all right?"

"More or less."

"Be quiet!"

She jumped at the sharp command, but realized immediately that it was aimed at Button. Thankfully, the shih tzu recognized the voice of authority. His annoying, high-pitched yelps subsided to muttered growls.

Swinging his attention back to Sheryl, Button's handler studied her with an intentness that raised little goose bumps on her arms. She couldn't remember the last time a man had looked at her like this, as though he wanted not just to see her, but into her. In fact, she couldn't remember the last time any man had *ever* looked at her like this. Brian certainly didn't. He was too considerate, too polite to make someone feel all prickly by such scrutiny.

"What can I do for you, Miss…?"

"Hancock. Sheryl Hancock. I know your aunt," she offered by way of explanation. "I just came by to check on her."

Those golden brown eyes lasered into her. "You know my aunt?"

"Yes. You're Paul Gunderson, aren't you?"

He was silent for a moment, then countered with a question of his own. "What makes you think so?"

"The mustache," she said with a tentative smile. And the thigh-hugging jeans, she added silently. "Your aunt talks about you all the time."

"Does she?"

"Yes. She's really proud of how well you're doing in the import-export business." Belatedly, Sheryl recalled the purpose of her visit. "Is she okay? I was worried when I didn't see her for a day or two."

"Inga's fine," he replied after a small pause. "She's upstairs. Resting."

Sheryl didn't see how anyone could rest through Button's shrill yapping, but then, Mrs. Gunderson was used to it.

"Oh, good." She started for the porch steps. "Would you tell her I came by, and that I'll talk to her tomorrow or whenever?"

Paul moved to one side. It was only a half step, a casual movement, but Sheryl couldn't edge past him without crowding against the wrought-iron rail.

"Why don't you come inside for a few minutes?" he suggested. "You can give me the real lowdown on what my aunt has to say about me, and we can both get out of the heat for a few minutes."

"I wish I could, but I'm running late for an appointment."

"There's some iced tea in the fridge. And a platter of freshly baked cookies on the kitchen table."

"Well…"

The cookies decided it. And Button's pitiable little whine. Obviously unhappy at being wedged into Paul's armpit, the dog snuffled noisily through its pug nose. The rhinestone-studded, bow-shaped barrette that kept his facial fur out of his eyes had slipped to one side. His bulging black orbs beseeched Sheryl to end his indignity.

She felt sorry for him but didn't make the mistake of reaching for the little stinker. The one time she'd tried to pet him at the post office, he'd nipped her fingers. As he now tried to nip Paul's. His sharp little teeth just missed the hand that brushed a tad too close to him. With a muttered oath, Paul jerked his hand away.

"How anyone could keep a noisy, bad-tempered fur ball like this as a pet is beyond me."

Somehow, the fact that Inga Gunderson's nephew disliked his aunt's obnoxious little Button made Sheryl feel as though they were allies of sorts. Smiling, she accepted his invitation and preceded him into the house.

Cool air wrapped around her like a sponge. The rooftop swamp cooler, so necessary to combat Albuquerque's dry, high-desert air, was obviously working overtime. As Sheryl's eyes made the adjustment from blazing outside light to the shadowed interior, she looked about in some surprise. The house certainly didn't fit Mrs. Gunderson's personality. No pictures decorated the walls. No knick-knacks crowded the tables. The furniture was a sort of pseudo-Southwest, a mix of bleached wood and brown Naugahyde, and not particularly comfortable looking.

Turning, she caught a glint of sunlight on Paul's dark hair as he bent down to deposit Button on the floor. To her consternation, she also caught a glimpse of what looked very much like a shoulder holster under the tan sport coat. She must have made some startled sound, because Paul glanced up and saw the direction of her wide-eyed stare. He released the dog and straightened, rolling his shoulders so that his jacket fell in place. The leather harness disappeared from view.

Sheryl had seen it, though.

And he knew she had.

His face went tight and altogether too hard for her peace of mind. Then Button gave a shrill, piercing bark and raced across the room. With another earsplitting yip, he disappeared up the stairs. He left behind a tense silence, broken only by the whoosh of chilled air being forced through the vents by the swamp cooler.

Sheryl swallowed a sudden lump in her throat. "Is that a gun under your jacket?"

"It is."

"I, uh, didn't know the import-export business was so risky."

"It can be."

She took a discreet step toward the door. Guns made her nervous. Very nervous. Even when carried by handsome strangers. Especially when carried by handsome strangers.

"I think I'll pass on the cookies. It's been a long day, and I'm late for an appointment. Tell your aunt that I'll see her tomorrow. Or whenever."

"I'd really like you to stay a few minutes, Miss Hancock. I'm anxious to hear what Inga has to say about her nephew."

"Some other time, maybe."

He stepped sideways, blocking her retreat as effectively as he had on the porch. But this time the movement wasn't the least casual.

"I'm afraid I'll have to insist."

Chapter 2

She knew about Inga Gunderson's nephew!

As he stared down into the blonde's wide, distinctly nervous green eyes, Deputy U.S. Marshal Harry MacMillan's pulse kicked up to twice its normal speed. He forgot about the ache in his gut, legacy of a roundhouse punch delivered by the seemingly frail, white-haired woman upstairs. He ignored the stinging little dents in his calf, courtesy of her sharp-toothed dust mop. His blood hammering, he gave the new entry onto the scene a thoroughly professional once-over.

Five-six or -seven, he guessed. A local, from her speech pattern and deep tan. As Harry had discovered in the week he'd been in Albuquerque, the sun carried twice the firepower at these mile-high elevations than it did at lower levels. It had certainly added a glow to this woman's skin. With her long, curly, corn-silk hair, tip-tilted nose and nicely proportioned set of curves, she looked more like the girl next door than the accomplice of an escaped fugitive. But Harry had been a U.S. marshal long enough to know that even the most angelic face could disguise the soul of a killer.

His jaw clenched at the memory of his friend's agonizing death. For a second or two, Harry debated whether to identify himself or milk more information from the woman first. He wasn't about to jeopardize this case, which had become a personal quest, by letting a suspect incriminate herself without Mirandizing her, but this woman wasn't a suspect. Yet.

"Tell me how you know Inga Gunderson."

Her eyes slid past him to the door. "I, uh, see her almost every day."

"Where?"

"At the branch office where I work."

"What branch office?"

She started to answer, then forced a deep, steadying breath into her lungs. "What's this all about? Is Mrs. Gunderson really all right?"

She had guts. Harry would give her that. She was obviously frightened. He could detect a faint tremor in the hands clenched at the seams of her navy shorts. Yet instead of replying to Harry's abrupt demands for information, she was throwing out a few questions of her own.

"Are you her nephew or not?"

He couldn't withhold his identity in the face of a direct question. Lifting his free hand, he reached into his coat pocket. The woman uttered a yelp every bit as piercing as the damned dog's, and jumped back.

"Relax, I'm just getting my ID."

He pulled out the worn brown-leather case containing his credentials. Flipping it open one-handed, he displayed the five-pointed gold star and a picture ID.

"Harry MacMillan, deputy U.S. marshal."

Her gaze swung from him to the badge to him and back again. Her nervousness gave way to a flash of indignation.

"Why didn't you say so?!"

"I just did." Coolly, he returned the case to his pocket. "May I see your identification, please."

"Mine? Why? I've told you my name."

Her response came out clipped and more than a little angry. That was fine with Harry. Until he discovered her exact relationship to the fugitive he'd been tracking for almost a year, he didn't mind keeping her rattled and off balance.

"I know who you said you were, Miss Hancock. I'd just like to see some confirmation."

"I left my purse in the car."

"Oh, that's smart."

The caustic comment made her stiffen, but before she could reply Harry cut back to the matter that had consumed his days and nights for so many months.

"Tell me again how you know Inga Gunderson."

Sheryl had always thought of herself as a dedicated federal employee. She enjoyed her job, and considered the service that she provided important to her community. Nor did she hesitate to volunteer her time and energies for special projects, such as selling T-shirts to aid victims of the devastating floods last year or coordinating the Christmas Wish program that responded to some of the desperate letters to Santa Claus that came into the post office during the holidays. She'd never come close to any kind of dangerous activity or bomb threats, but she certainly would have cooperated with other federal agencies in any ongoing investigation…if asked.

What nicked the edges of her normally placid temper was that this man didn't ask. He demanded. Still, he was a federal agent. And he wanted an answer.

"Mrs. Gunderson stops in almost every day at the station where I work," she repeated.

"What station?"

"The Monzano Street post office."

"The Monzano post office." He shoved a hand through his short, cinnamon-brown hair. "Well, hell!"

Sheryl bristled at the unbridled disgust in his voice. Although her friendly personality and ready smile acted as a preventive against the verbal abuse many postal employees experienced, she'd endured her share of sneers and jokes about the post office. The slurs, even said in fun, always hurt. She took pride in her work, as did most of her co-workers. What's more, she'd chosen a demanding occupation. She'd like to see anyone, this lean, tough deputy marshal included, sling the amount of mail she did each day and still come up smiling.

"Do you have a problem with the post office?" she asked with a touch of belligerence.

"What?" The question seemed to jerk him from his private and not very pleasant thoughts. "No. Have a seat, Miss Hancock. I'll call my contacts and verify your identity."

"Why?" she asked again.

His hawk's eyes sliced into her. "You've just walked into the middle of an ongoing investigation. You're not walking out until I ascertain that you're who you say you are…and until I understand your exact relationship with the woman who calls herself 'Mrs. Gunderson.'"

"*Calls* herself 'Inga Gunderson'?"

"Among other aliases. Sit down."

Feeling a little like Alice sliding down through the rabbit hole, Sheryl perched on the edge of the uncomfortable, sand-colored sofa. Good grief! What in the world had she stumbled into?

She found out a few moments later. Deputy U.S. Marshal MacMillan dropped the phone onto its cradle and ran a quick, assessing eye over her yellow tank top and navy shorts.

"Well, you check out. The FBI's computers have your weight at 121, but the rest of the details from your background information file substantiate your identity."

Sheryl wasn't sure which flustered her more, the fact that this man had instant access to her background file or that he'd accurately noted the few extra pounds she'd put on recently. Okay, more than a few pounds.

MacMillan's gaze swept over her once more, then settled on her face. "According to the file, you're clean. Not even a speeding ticket in the past ten years."

From his dry tone, he didn't consider a spotless driving record a particularly meritorious achievement.

"Thank you. I think. Now will you tell me what's

going on here? Is Mrs. Gunderson…or whoever she is…really all right? Why in the world is a deputy U.S. marshal checking up on that sweet, fragile lady?"

"Because we suspect that sweet, fragile lady of being involved in the illegal importation of depleted uranium."

"Mrs. *Gunderson?*"

The marshal, Sheryl decided, had been sniffing something a lot more potent than the glue on the back of stamps!

"Let me get this straight. You think Inga Gunderson is smuggling uranium?"

"Depleted uranium," he corrected, as though she should know the difference.

She didn't.

"It's the same heavy metal that's used in the manufacture of armor-piercing artillery shells," he explained in answer to her blank look. Almost imperceptibly, his voice roughened. "Recently, it's also been used to produce new cop-killer bullets."

Sheryl stared at him, stunned. For the life of her, she couldn't connect the tiny, chirpy woman who brought her and her co-workers mouthwatering spice cakes with a smuggling ring. A uranium smuggling ring, for heaven's sake! Of all the thoughts whirling around in her confused, chaotic mind, only one surfaced.

"I thought the Customs Service tracked down smugglers."

"They do." The planes of MacMillan's face became merciless. "We're working with Customs on this, as well as with the Nuclear Regulatory Commission, the FBI, the CIA and a whole alphabet of other agencies on this case. But the U.S. Marshals Service has a special interest in the outcome of this case. One of our deputies took a uranium-tipped bullet in the chest when he was escorting Inga Gunderson's supposed nephew to prison."

"Paul?" Sheryl gasped.

The hazy image she'd formed of a handsome, mustached jet-setter lazing on the beach at Ipanema among the bikinied Brazilians surfaced for a moment, then shattered forever.

She shook her head in dismay. She should have known better than to let herself become intrigued, even slightly, by a globe-trotting wanderer! Her father hadn't stayed in one place long enough for anyone, her mother included, to get to know him or his many varied business concerns. For all Sheryl knew, he could have been a smuggler, too. But not, she prayed, a murderer.

At the memory of her father's roving ways, she gave silent, heartfelt thanks for her steady, reliable, soon-to-be-fiancé. Sure, Brian occasionally fell asleep on the couch beside her. And once or twice he'd displayed more excitement over the prospect of closing a real estate deal than he did over their plans for the future. But Sheryl knew he would always be there for her.

As he was probably there for her right now, she realized with a start. No doubt he was waiting in the heat at the house he wanted to show her, flicking impatient little glances at his watch. She'd promised to be there by three-thirty. She snuck a quick look at her watch. It was well past that now, she saw.

"What do you know about Paul Gunderson?"

The curt question snapped her attention back to Deputy Marshal MacMillan.

"Only what Inga told me. That he's a sales rep for an international firm and that he travels a lot. From his postcards, it looks like his company sends him to some pretty exotic locales."

MacMillan dropped his hands from his hips. His well-muscled body seemed to torque to an even higher degree of tension.

"Postcards?" he asked softly.

"He sends her bright, cheery cards from the various places he travels to. They come to her box at the Monzano branch. We—my friends at the post office and I—thought it was sweet the way he stayed in touch with his aunt like that."

"Yeah, real sweet." His face tight with disgust, Mac-Millan shook his head. "We ordered a mail cover the same day we tracked Inga Gunderson to Albuquerque. The folks at the central post office assured us they had the screen in place. Dammit, they should have caught the fact that she had another postal box."

Sheryl's defensive hackles went up on behalf of her fellow employees. "Hey, they're only human. They do their best."

The marshal didn't dignify that with a reply. He thought for a moment, his forehead furrowed.

"We didn't find any postcards here at the house. Obviously, Inga Gunderson destroyed them as soon as she retrieved them from her box. Did you happen to see the messages on the cards?"

Sheryl squirmed a bit. Technically, postal employees weren't supposed to read their patrons' mail. It was hard to abide by that rule, though. More than one of the male clerks slipped raunchy magazines out of their brown wrappers for a peek when the supervisors weren't around. *Cosmos* and *Good Housekeeping* had been known to take a detour to the ladies' room. The glossy postcards that came from all over the world weren't wrapped, though, and even the most conscientious employee, which Sheryl considered herself, couldn't resist a peek.

"Well, I may have glanced at one or two. Like the one that arrived this morning, for instance. It—"

The marshal started. "One came in this morning?"

"Yes. From Rio."

"Damn! Wait here. I'm going to get my partner." He spun on one booted heel. His long legs ate up the distance to the hallway. "Ev! Bring the woman down!"

Sheryl heard a terse reply, followed by a series of shrill yaps. A few moments later, she recognized Mrs. Gunderson's distinctive Scandinavian accent above the dog's clamor. When she made out the specific words, Sheryl's jaw sagged. She wouldn't have imagined that her smiling, white-haired patron could know such obscenities, much less spew them out like that!

She watched, wide-eyed, as a short, stocky man hauled a handcuffed Inga Gunderson into the living room.

"Get your hands off me, you fat little turd!"

The elderly lady accompanied her strident demand with a swing of her foot. A sturdy black oxford connected with her escort's left shin. Button connected with his right.

Luckily, the newcomer was wearing slacks. As Mac-Millan had earlier, he took several dancing hops, shaking his leg furiously to dislodge the little dog. Button hung on like a snarling, bug-eyed demon.

The law enforcement officer sent MacMillan a look of profound disgust. "Shoot the damned thing, will you?"

"No!"

Both women uttered the protest simultaneously. As much as Sheryl disliked the spoiled, noisy shih tzu, she didn't want to see it hurt.

"Button!" she commanded. "Down, boy!"

The dog ignored Sheryl's order, but its black eyes rolled to one side at the sound of its mistress's frantic pleas.

"Let go, precious. Let go, and come to Mommy."

The warbly, pleading voice was so different from the one that had been spitting vile oaths just moments ago that both men blinked. Sheryl, who'd heard Inga Gunderson carry on lengthy, cooing conversations with her pet many times before, wasn't as surprised by the abrupt transition from vitriol to syrupy sweetness.

"Let go, sweetie-kins. Come to Mommy."

The shih tzu released its death grip on the agent's pants.

"There's a pretty Butty-boo."

With his black eyes still hostile under the lopsided rhinestone hair clip, the little dog settled on its haunches beside its mistress. In another disconcerting shift in both tone and temperament, Inga Gunderson directed her attention to Sheryl.

"What are you doing here? Don't tell me you're working with these pigs, too?"

"No. That is, I just stopped by to make sure you were all right and I—"

"She's been telling us about some postcards," Mac-Millan interrupted ruthlessly.

Inga's seamed face contorted. Fury blazed in her black eyes. "You just waltzed in here and started spilling your guts to these jerks? Is that the thanks I get for baking all those damn cookies for you and the other idiots at the post office, so you wouldn't lose my mail like you do everyone else's?"

Shocked, Sheryl had no reply. Even Button seemed taken aback by his mistress's venom. He gave an uncertain whine, as if unsure whom he should attack this time. Before he could decide, MacMillan reached down and once again scooped the dog into the tight, restraining pocket of his arm.

"Get her out of here," he ordered his partner curtly. "Call for backup and wait in the car until it arrives. I'll meet you at the detention facility when I finish with Miss Hancock."

The older woman spit out another oath as she was tugged toward the front door. "Hancock can't tell you anything. She doesn't know a thing. *I* don't know a thing! If you think you can pin a smuggling rap on me, you're pumping some of that coke you feds like to snitch whenever you seize a load."

Yipping furiously, Button tried to squirm free of the marshal's hold and go after his mistress. MacMillan waited until the slam of the front door cut off most of Mrs. Gunderson's angry protests before releasing the dog. Nails clicking on the wood floor, the animal dashed for the hallway. His grating, high-pitched barks rose to a crescendo as his claws scratched frantically at the door.

Sheryl shut out the dog's desperate cries and focused, instead, on the man who faced her, his eyes watchful behind their screen of gold-tipped lashes.

"She's right. I don't know anything. Nothing that pertains to uranium smuggling, anyway."

"Why don't you let me decide what is and isn't pertinent? Tell me again about these postcards."

"There's nothing to tell, really. They come in spurts, every few weeks, from different places around the world. The messages are brief—from the little I've noticed of them," Sheryl tacked on hastily.

"Can you remember dates to go with the locations?"

"Maybe. If I think about it."

"Good! I want to take a look at the card that arrived this morning. If you don't mind, we can take your car back to the branch office."

"Now?"

"Now."

"But I have an appointment."

"Cancel it."

"You don't understand. I'm supposed to meet my fiancé."

The marshal's keen gaze took in her ringless left hand, then lifted to her face.

"We're, uh, unofficially engaged," Sheryl explained for the second time that day.

"This shouldn't take long," MacMillan assured her, taking her elbow to guide her toward the door. "You can use my cell phone to call your friend."

His touch felt warm on her skin and decidedly firm. They made it to the hall before a half whine, half growl stopped them both in their tracks. The shih tzu blocked the front door, his black eyes uncertain under his silky black-and-white fur.

"We can't just leave Button," Sheryl protested.

"I'll have someone contact the animal shelter. They can pick him up."

"The shelter?" Her brows drew together. "They only keep animals for a week or so. What happens if Mrs. Gunderson isn't free to claim him within the allotted time?"

"We'll make sure they keep the mutt as long as necessary."

A touch of impatience colored MacMillan's deep voice. He reached for the door, and the dog gave another uncertain whine. Sheryl dragged her feet, worrying her lower lip with her teeth.

"He doesn't understand what's happening."

"Yeah, well, he'll figure things out soon enough if he tries to take a chunk out of the animal control people."

"I take it you're not a dog lover, Mr....Sheriff... Marshal MacMillan."

"Call me 'Harry.' And, yes, I like dogs. Real dogs. Not hairy little rats wearing rhinestones. Now, if you don't mind, Miss Hancock, I'd like to get to the post office and take a look at that postcard."

"We can't just let him be carted off to the pound."

The marshal's jaw squared. "I don't think you understand the seriousness of this investigation. A law enforcement officer died, possibly because of Inga Gunderson's complicity in illegal activity."

"I'm sorry," she said quietly. "But that's not Button's fault."

"I didn't say it was."

"We can't just leave him."

"Yes, we can."

With her sunny disposition and easygoing nature, Sheryl didn't find it necessary to dig in her heels very often. But when she did, they stayed dug.

"I won't leave him."

Some moments later, Sheryl stepped out of the adobe house into the suffocating heat. A disgruntled deputy U.S. marshal trailed behind her, carrying an equally disgruntled shih tzu under his arm.

She slid into her car and winced as the oven-hot vinyl seat covers singed the backs of her thighs. Trying to keep the smallest possible portion of her anatomy in direct contact with the seat, she keyed the ignition and shoved the air-conditioning to max.

With the two males eyeing each other warily in the passenger seat, Sheryl retraced the route to the Monzano station. She was pulling into the parking lot behind the building when she realized that she'd forgotten all about Brian. She started to ask Harry MacMillan if she could use his phone, but he had already climbed out.

He came around the car in a few man-sized strides. Opening her door, he reached down a hand to help Sheryl out. The courteous gesture from the sharp-edged marshal surprised her. Tentatively, her fingers folded around MacMillan's hand. It was harder than Brian's, she thought with a little tingle of awareness that took her by surprise. Rougher. Like the man himself.

Swinging out of the car, she tugged her hand free with a small smile of thanks. "We can go in the back door. I have the combination."

Button went with them, of course. They couldn't leave him in the car. Even this late in the afternoon, heat shimmered like clear, wavery smoke above the asphalt. Stuffed once more under MacMillan's arm and distinctly unhappy about it, the little dog snuffled indignantly through his pug nose.

Sweat trickled down between Sheryl's breasts by the time she punched the combination into the cipher lock and led the way into the dim, cavernous interior. Familiar gray walls and a huge expanse of black tile outlined with bright-yellow tape to mark the work areas welcomed her. As anxious now as MacMillan to retrieve the postcard from Mrs. Gunderson's box, she wove her way among hampers stacked high with outgoing mail toward her supervisor's desk, situated strategically in the center of the work area.

"You do have a search warrant, don't you?" she asked Harry over one shoulder.

He nodded confidently. "We have authority to screen all mail sent to the address of Inga Gunderson, alias Betty Hoffman, alias Eva Jorgens."

"Her home address or her post office box?"

"Does it make a difference?"

At MacMillan's frown, Sheryl stopped. "You need specific authority to search a post office box."

"I'm sure the warrant includes that authority."

"We'll have to verify that fact."

Impatience flickered in his eyes. "Let's talk to your supervisor about it."

"We will. I'd have to get her approval before I could allow you into the box in any case."

Sheryl introduced Harry to Pat Martinez, a tall, willowy Albuquerque native with jet-black hair dramatically winged in silver. The customer service supervisor obligingly called the main post office and requested a copy of the warrant. It whirred up on the fax a few moments later.

After ripping it off the machine, Pat skimmed through it. "I'm sorry, this isn't specific enough. It only grants you authority to search mail addressed to Mrs. Gunderson's home address. It'll have to be amended to allow access to a postal box."

Sheryl politely kept any trace of "I told you so" off her face. Harry wasn't as restrained. He scowled at her boss with distinct displeasure.

"Are you sure?"

"Yes, Marshal, I'm sure," Pat drawled. With twenty-two years of service under her belt, she would be. "But you're welcome to call the postal inspector at the central office for confirmation."

He conceded defeat with a distinct lack of graciousness. "I'll take your word for it." Still scowling, he shoved Button at Sheryl. "Here, hold your friend."

He pulled a small black address book out of his pocket, then punched a number into the phone. His face tight, he asked the person who answered at the other end about the availability of a federal judge named, appropriately, Warren. He listened intently for a moment, then requested that the speaker dispatch a car and driver to the Monzano Street post office immediately.

Sheryl watched him hang up with a mixture of relief and regret. Her part in the unfolding Mrs. Gunderson drama was over. She certainly didn't want to get any more involved with smugglers and kindly old ladies who spewed obscenities, but the trip to Inga's house had certainly livened up her day. So had the broad-shouldered law enforcement officer. Sheryl couldn't wait to tell Brian and Elise about her brush with the U.S. Marshals Service.

MacMillan soon disabused her of the notion that her role in what she privately termed the post office caper had ended, however.

"I'll be back in forty-five minutes," he told her curtly. "An hour at most. I'm sorry, but I'll have to ask you to wait for me here."

"Me? Why?"

"I want you to take a look at the message on this postcard and tell me how it compares with the others."

"But I'm already late for my appointment."

He cocked his head, studying her with a glint in his eyes that Sheryl couldn't quite interpret.

"Just out of curiosity, do you always make appointments, not dates, with this guy you're sort of engaged to?"

Since the question was entirely too personal and none of his business, she ignored it. "I'm late," she repeated firmly. "I have to go."

"You're a material witness in a federal investigation, Miss Hancock. If I have to, I'll get a subpoena from Judge Warren while I'm downtown and bring you in for questioning."

She hitched Button up on her hip, eyeing MacMillan with a good deal less than friendliness.

"You know, Marshal, your bedside manner could use a little work."

"I'm a law enforcement officer, not a doctor," he reminded her. Unnecessarily, she thought. Then, to her astonishment, his mustache lifted in a quick, slashing grin.

"But this is the first time I've had any complaints about my bedside manner. Just wait for me here, okay? And don't talk about the case to anyone else until I get back."

Sheryl was still feeling the impact of that toe-curling grin when Harry MacMillan strode out of the post office a few moments later.

Chapter 3

With only a little encouragement, the Albuquerque police officer detailed to Harry's special fugitive task force got him to the Dennis Chavez Federal Building in seventeen minutes flat. Luckily, they pushed against the rush-hour traffic streaming out of downtown Albuquerque and the huge air force base just south of I-40. The car had barely rolled to a stop at the rear entrance to the federal building before Harry had the door open.

"Thanks."

"Any time, Marshal. Always happy to help out a Wyatt Earp who's lost his horse."

Grinning at the reference to the most legendary figure of the U.S. Marshals Service, Harry tipped him a two-fingered salute. A moment later, he flashed his credentials at the courthouse security checkpoint. The guard obligingly turned off the sensors of the metal detector to accommodate his weapon and waved him through.

Harry took the stairs to the judge's private chambers two at a time. Despite his impatience over this detour downtown for another warrant, excitement whipped through him. He was close. So damned close. With a sixth sense honed by his fifteen years as a U.S. marshal, Harry could almost see the fugitive he'd been tracking for the past eleven months. Hear him panting in fear. Smell his stink.

Paul Gunderson. Aka Harvey Millard and Jacques Garone and Rafael Pasquale and a half-dozen other aliases. Harry knew him in every one of his assumed personas. The bastard had started life as Richard Johnson. Had gone all through high school and college and a good part of a government career with that identity. His performance record as an auditor for the Defense Department described him as well above average in intelligence but occasionally stubborn and difficult to supervise. So difficult, apparently, that a long string of bosses had failed to question the necessity for his frequent trips abroad.

While conducting often unnecessary audits of overseas units, Johnson had also used his string of aliases to establish a very lucrative side business as a broker for the sale and shipment of depleted uranium, a by-product of the nuclear process. As Harry had discovered, most of the uranium Johnson illegally diverted went to arms manufacturers who used it to produce armor-piercing artillery and mortar shells for sale to third-world countries. But recently a new type of handgun ammunition had made an appearance on the black market, and the U.S. government had mounted a special task force to find its source.

When he was arrested a little over two years ago, Johnson had claimed that he didn't know the product he brokered was being used to manufacture bullets that shredded police officers' protective armor like confetti. The man who gunned down the marshals escorting Johnson to trial certainly knew, though. He left one officer writhing in agony. In the ensuing melee, Johnson finished off the other.

Harry had lost a friend that day. His best friend.

He'd been tracking Johnson ever since. After months of frustrating dead ends, chance information from a snitch had established a tenuous link between Johnson and the Gunderson woman. She'd slipped through their fingers several times before Harry finally traced her to Albuquerque. Through the damned dog yet! Harry didn't even want to think about all the calls they'd made to veterinarians and grooming parlors before they got a lead on an elderly woman with a Scandinavian accent and a black-and-white shih tzu!

They'd no sooner found her than she'd almost slipped away again. Harry had barely set up electronic surveillance of her home when the same dog groomer who IDed her alerted him that Inga Gunderson had canceled her pet's regularly scheduled appointment. She was, according to the groomer, going out of town. Harry had been forced to move in…and had gotten nothing out of the woman.

Then Sheryl Hancock had stumbled on the scene.

With her tumble of blond hair and sunshine-filled green eyes, she would have made Harry's pulse jump in the most ordinary of circumstances. The fact that she provided a definitive link to Paul Gunderson sent it shooting right off the Richter scale. He shook his head, still not quite believing that the Gundersons had been using the U.S. mail to coordinate their activities all this time.

The mail, for God's sake!

In retrospect, he supposed it made sense. Phones were too easily tapped these days. Radio and satellite communications too frequently intercepted by scanners set to random searches of the airwaves. For all the heat the postal system sometimes took, it usually delivered…which was more than could be said for a good many other institutions, private or public. The card sitting in Inga Gunderson's box right now could very well hold vital information. Every nerve in Harry's body tightened at the thought of studying its message.

He cornered the judge and did some fast talking to obtain an amended warrant. A quick call to his partner to check on Inga Gunderson's status confirmed what Harry already suspected. The woman refused to talk until her lawyer arrived. Since the man was currently cruising the interstate somewhere on the other side of Amarillo, it would be some hours yet before he arrived and they could confront the suspect.

"Everything we've got on her is circumstantial," Ev warned. "I don't know if it's enough to hold her unless we establish a hard connection between her and Richard Johnson or Paul Gunderson or whatever he's calling himself now."

"I'm working on it. Just sit on the woman as hard as you can. Maybe she'll crack. And give me a call when her lawyer shows."

"Will do."

Harry hung up, more determined than ever to get his hands on that postcard.

"Box 89212?"

Buck Aguilar glanced from Sheryl and Pat Martinez to the man facing him across a sorting rack. Oblivious to the tension radiating from the marshal, the postal worker handed Pat back the amended warrant.

"Closed that box this afternoon."

He picked up the stack of mail he'd been working before the interruption. Letters flew in a white blur into the sorting bins.

His face a study in disbelief, Harry leaned forward. "What do you mean, you closed it?"

At the fierce demand, Buck lifted his head once again. Slowly, his gaze drifted from the marshal's face to his boots and back up again. From the expression on the mail carrier's broad, sculpted face, Sheryl could tell that he didn't take kindly to being grilled.

"Got a notice terminating the box," Buck replied in his taciturn way. "Closed it."

The clatter of wheels on concrete as another employee pushed a cart across the room drowned Harry's short, explicit reply. Sheryl caught the gist of it, though. The marshal was *not* happy. She waited for the fireworks. They weren't long in coming.

"What did you do with the contents of the box? Or more specifically—" Harry sent a dagger glance at Sheryl and her supervisor "—what did you do with the postcard that was in there?"

"Returned to sender. Had to. BCNO."

"What the hell does that mean?"

Buck glanced at the marshal again, his eyes flat. Spots of red rose in his cheeks, darkening the skin he'd inherited from his Jacarillo Apache ancestors. Sheryl and the other employees at the Monzano branch office knew that look. Too well. It settled on her co-worker's face whenever he was about to butt heads with another employee or an obnoxious customer. Since Buck stood six-four and carried close to 250 pounds on his muscled frame, that didn't occur often. But when it did, the results weren't pretty.

Pat Martinez replied for him. "*BCNO* means 'Box closed, no order.' Without a forwarding order, we have no choice but to return the mail to sender."

"Dammit!"

"You got a problem with that, Sheriff?"

Buck's soft query lifted the hairs on Sheryl's neck.

"Yeah, I've got a problem with that. And it's 'Marshal.'"

The two men faced each other across the bin like characters in some B-grade Western movie. *The Lawman and the Apache.* At any minute, Sheryl expected them to whip out their guns and knives. Even Button sensed the sudden tension. Poking his nose through the straps of Sheryl's purse, he issued a low, throaty growl.

Hastily, she stepped into the breech. "Maybe it's not too late to retrieve the card. What time did you close the box, Buck?"

His gaze shifted once again. Infinitesimally, his expression softened. "'Bout three-thirty, Sher."

"Oh, dear."

Although it seemed impossible, the marshal bristled even more. "What does 'oh, dear' mean?"

She turned to him, apology spilling from her green eyes. "I'm afraid it means that the contents of Mrs. Gunderson's box went back to the Processing and Distribution Center on the four o'clock run."

"You mean that postcard left here even before I went chasing downtown after the blasted amended warrant?"

"Well…yes."

Harry stared at her, aggravation apparent in every line of his body. For a moment, she wasn't quite sure how he'd handle this new setback. Finally, he blew out a long, ragged breath.

"So where is this distribution center?"

"The P&DC is on Broadway, but…"

"But what?"

Sheryl shared a look with her supervisor and co-worker. They were more than willing to let her handle the thoroughly disgruntled marshal. Bracing herself, she gave him the bad news.

"But the center uses state-of-the-art, high-speed sorters. It also makes runs to the airport every half hour. Since we rent cargo space on all the commercial carriers, your postcard would have gone out—" she glanced at the clock on the wall "—an hour ago, at least. Depending on how it was routed, it's halfway to Dallas or Atlanta or New York right now."

A muscle twitched on the side of MacMillan's jaw. "I suppose there's no way to trace the routing?"

"Not unless it was certified, registered or sent via Global Express, which it wasn't."

"Great!"

A heavy silence descended, broken when Pat Martinez handed Harry his useless warrant.

"I'm sorry about sending you downtown on a wild-goose chase, Marshal, but I won't apologize for the fact that my employees followed regulations. If you don't need me for anything else, I'll get back to work."

"No. Thanks."

Buck moved off, too, rolling his empty hamper away to collect a full one from the row at the back of the box area. Sheryl and Button waited while Harry rubbed a hand across the back of his neck, flattening his cotton shirt against his stomach and ribs.

At the sight of those lean hollows and broad surfaces, a sudden and completely unexpected tingle of aware-ness darted through Sheryl. Content with Brian, she hadn't looked at other men in the year or so they'd been dating. She'd certainly never let her gaze linger on a set of washboard ribs or a flat, trim belly. Or noticed the tight fit of a pair of jeans across muscled thighs and…

"Are you hungry?"

Sheryl jerked her gaze upward. "Excuse me?"

"Are you hungry? I skipped breakfast, and Ev and I

were too busy taking physical and verbal abuse from the Gunderson woman to grab lunch. Why don't we have dinner while we talk about these postcards?"

"Tonight?"

The tightness left his face. A corner of his thick, luxuriant mustache tipped up in a reluctant smile. "That was the general idea. I know I made you miss your… appointment…with this guy you're sort of engaged to. Let me make it up to you by feeding you while I squeeze your brain."

"Squeeze my brain, huh? Interesting approach. Does it get you a lot of dinner dates?"

"It never fails." His smile feathered closer to a grin. "Another example of my charming bedside manner, Miss Hancock. So, are you hungry?"

She was starved, Sheryl realized. She was also obligated to provide what information she could to the authorities, represented in this instance by Deputy U.S. Marshal Harry MacMillan.

Still, she hesitated. When she'd called Brian a while ago to apologize for standing him up, he'd sounded more than a little piqued. Sheryl couldn't blame him. In an attempt to soothe his ruffled feathers, she'd promised to cook his favorite chicken dish tonight. They'd fallen into the routine of eating at her apartment on Tuesdays and his on Fridays. This was supposed to have been her night. Oh, well, she'd just have to make it up to him next week.

"I need to make a phone call," she said, hitching her purse and its furry passenger up on her shoulder.

Graciously, MacMillan handed her his mobile

phone. With both dog and man listening in, Sheryl conducted a short, uncomfortable conversation with Brian.

"I'm sorry I've kept you waiting all this time, but something's come up. I'm going to be tied up awhile longer. Yes, I know it's Tuesday night. No, I can't put this off until tomorrow."

She caught MacMillan's speculative gaze, and turned a shoulder. "Yes. Maybe. I'll phone you when I get home."

Sheryl ended the call on a small sigh. Brian's structured approach to life usually gave her such a comfortable feeling. Sometimes, though, it made things just a bit difficult.

"Trouble in almost-paradise?" Harry inquired politely, slipping his phone back into his pocket.

"Not really. Where would you like to eat?"

"You pick it. I don't know Albuquerque all that well."

She thought for a minute. "How about El Pinto? They have the best Mexican food in the city and we can get a table outside, where we can talk privately."

"Sounds good to me."

Sheryl led the way to the rear exit, absorbing the fact that he was apparently a stranger to the city.

"Where's home? Or can you say?"

As soon as she articulated the casual question, she wondered if he would…or should…answer. She had no idea what kind of security U.S. marshals operated under. He'd told her not to talk about the case. Maybe he wasn't supposed to talk about himself, either.

Evidently, that wasn't a problem.

"I'm assigned to the fugitive apprehension unit of the

Oklahoma City district office," he replied, "but I don't spend a whole lot of time there. My job keeps me on the road most of the time."

Another wanderer! They seemed to constitute half the world's population. Sheryl's minor annoyance with Brian's inflexibility vanished instantly. He, at least, wouldn't take off without warning for parts unknown. She led the way outside, blinking at the abrupt transition from dim interior to dazzling sunlight.

"I'd better meet you at the restaurant. I'll have to go by my apartment first to drop off Button. Unless you want to take him back to your place?" she finished hopefully.

"I can't," he replied without the slightest hint of regret. "I'm staying in a motel."

She sighed, resigning herself to an unplanned houseguest. "Do you know how to get to El Pinto?"

"Haven't got a clue. Just give me the address. I'll find it."

She chewed her lip, thinking perhaps she should suggest a more accessible place. "It's kind of hard to locate if you're not familiar with Albuquerque."

He sent her a look of patented amusement. "U.S. marshals have been tracking down bad guys since George Washington pinned gold stars on the original thirteen deputies. I'm pretty sure I can find this restaurant."

"I stand corrected," Sheryl said gravely.

She drove out of the parking lot a few moments later, with Button occupying the seat beside her. Harry trailed in a tan government sedan. Following her directions, he turned south at the corner of Haines and Juan Tabo, and she headed north.

By this late hour, Albuquerque's rush-hour traffic had thinned to a steady but fast-moving stream. The trip to her apartment complex took less than fifteen minutes. As always, the cream-colored adobe architecture and profusion of flowers decorating the fountain in the center of the tree-shaded complex gave her a quiet joy. Sheryl had moved into her one-bedroom apartment soon after her last promotion and loved its cool Southwestern colors and high-ceilinged rooms. It was perfect for her, but the pale-mauve carpet hadn't been pet-proofed. After unlocking the front door, she set the shih tzu down in the tiled foyer.

"We have to establish a few ground rules, fella. No yapping, or you'll get me thrown out of here. No taking bites out of me or my furniture. No accidents on the rug."

Busy sniffing out the place, Button ignored her.

"I'm serious," she warned.

Once she'd plopped her purse down on the counter separating the kitchen from the small dining area, she pulled a plastic bowl from the cupboard and filled it with water.

"It's either me or the pound, so you'd better… Hey!"

With regal indifference to her startled protest, the shih tzu lifted his raised leg another inch and sprayed the dining table.

Obviously, Button didn't believe in rules!

Sheryl went to work with paper towels, then scooped up the unrepentant dog. A moment later, she set him and the water dish down on the other side of the sliding-glass patio doors. Hands on hips, she surveyed the small, closed-in area. The leafy Chinese elm growing on the other side of the adobe wall provided plenty of shade. The few square yards of grass edging the patio tiles provided Button's other necessary commodity.

"This is your temporary residence, dog. Make yourself comfortable."

After sliding the patio door closed behind her, she heeled off her sneakers and padded into the bathroom to splash cold water on her face. Then she shucked her shorts and tank top and pulled on a gauzy sundress in a cool mint green. She had her hair unbraided and was pulling a brush through its stubborn curls when a series of high-pitched yips told her Button wanted in.

Too bad. He'd better get used to outdoor living.

She soon learned that what Button wanted, Button had his own way of getting. Within moments, the yips rose to a grating, insistent crescendo.

The brush hit the counter with a thud. Muttering, Sheryl retraced her steps and cut the dog's protests off with a stern admonition.

"I guess I didn't make myself clear. You've lost your house privileges. You're going to camp out here on the patio, Buttsy-boo, or take a trip to the pound."

Ten minutes later, Sheryl slammed the front door behind her and left a smug Button in undisputed possession of her air-conditioned apartment. It was either cave in to his hair-raising howls or risk eviction. In desperation, she'd spread a layer of newspapers over the bathroom floor. She could only hope that the dog would condescend to use them. The next few days, she thought grimly, could prove a severe strain on her benevolence toward animals in general and squish-faced lapdogs in particular.

As she shoved the car key into the ignition, a sudden thought struck her. If even half of what Harry had told her about Mrs. Gunderson's activities was true, Sheryl could be stuck with her unwanted houseguest for a lot longer than a few days.

Groaning, she backed out of the carport. No way was she keeping that mutt for more than a day or two. Harry had to have stumbled across some relative or acquaintance of Mrs. Gunderson during his investigation, someone who could take over custody of her pet. She put the issue on the table as soon as they were seated in El Pinto's shaded, colorful outdoor dining area. Harry stretched his long legs out under the tiled table and graciously refrained from pointing out that it was her insistence on taking the dog with them that had caused her dilemma in the first place.

"There's nothing I'd like better than to identify a few of Inga Gunderson's friends and acquaintances."

Sheryl had to scoot her chair closer to catch his reply over the noise of the busy restaurant. A fountain bubbled and splashed just behind them, providing a cheerful accompaniment to the mariachi trio strumming and thumping their guitars as they strolled through the patio area. Harry had chosen the table deliberately so they could talk without raising the interest of other diners. Even so, Sheryl hadn't counted on practically sitting in his lap to carry on a conversation.

"As far as we know," he continued, "Inga doesn't have any acquaintances here. She made a few calls to local businesses, but no one's phoned her or visited her." His gold-flecked eyes settled on his dinner partner. "Except you, Miss Hancock."

"'Sheryl,'" she amended absently. "So what will happen to her?"

"We have sufficient circumstantial evidence to book her on suspicion of smuggling. The charge might or might not stick, but she's not the one I really want. It's her supposed nephew I'm after."

Despite Harry's relaxed pose, Sheryl couldn't miss the utter implacability in his face. He slipped a pen and small black-leather notebook out of his jacket pocket, all business now.

"Tell me about the postcards."

She waited to reply until the waitress had placed a brimming basket of tortilla chips on the table and taken their drink orders.

"They usually come in batches," she told Harry. "Two or three will arrive within a week of each other, then a month might go by before another set comes in."

"I figured as much," the marshal said, almost to himself. "He'd have to send backups in case the first didn't arrive. Have any others come in with this one from Rio?"

"Two. The first was from Prague. The second from Pamplona."

"Pamplona?" His brow creased. "Isn't that where they run bulls through the streets? With the locals running right ahead of them?"

"That's what the scene on the card showed." Sheryl hunched forward, recalling the vivid street scene with a shake of her head. "Can you imagine racing down a narrow, cobbled street a few steps ahead of thundering, black bulls?"

"I can imagine it, but it's not real high on my list of fun things to do," Harry admitted dryly. He loaded a chip with salsa. "How about you?"

"Me? No way! I have enough trouble staying ahead of my bills, let alone a herd of bulls. Uh, you'd better go easy on that stuff. I heard the green chili crop came in especially hot this year."

"Not to fear, I've got a lead-lined stom— Arrggh!"

He shot up straight in his chair, grabbed his water glass and downed the entire contents in three noisy gulps. Blinking rapidly, he stared at the little dish of salsa in disbelief.

"Good Lord! Do you New Mexicans really eat this stuff?"

"Some of us do," Sheryl answered, laughing. "But we work up to it over a period of years."

The waitress arrived at that moment. Harry shot her a look of profound gratitude and all but snatched the Don Miguel light he'd ordered out of her hand. The ice-cold beer, like the water, went down in a few long, gulping swallows.

The waitress turned an amused smile on Sheryl. "Didn't you warn him?"

"I tried to."

Winking, she picked up her tray. "Another gringo bites the dust."

Sheryl eyed the marshal, not quite sure she'd agree with the waitress's assessment. His golden brown eyes watered, to be sure. A pepper-induced flush darkened his cheeks above the line of his mustache. He drained his mug with the desperation of a man who'd just crawled across a hundred miles of burning desert.

She would categorize him as down, but certainly not out. He showed too much strength in those broad shoulders. Carried himself with too much authority. Even in his boots and jeans and casual open-necked shirt, he gave the impression of a man who knew what he wanted and went after it.

For an unguarded moment, Sheryl wondered if he would pursue a woman he desired with the same single-minded determination he pursued the fugitives he hunted. He would, she decided. He'd pursue her, and when he caught her, he'd somehow manage to convince her she'd been the hunter all along. The thought sent a ripple of excitement singing through her veins. She shook her head at her own foolishness.

Still, the tingle stayed with her while Harry dragged the heel of his hand across his eyes.

"Remind me to listen to your warnings next time."

The offhand remark made Sheryl smile, until she realized that there probably wouldn't be a next time. As soon as she filled Marshal MacMillan in on the details from the postcards, he'd ride off into the sunset in pursuit of his quarry.

How stupid of her to romanticize his profession. She'd better remember that he lived the same life-style her father had. Here today, gone tomorrow, with never a backward glance for those he left behind.

Recovering from his bout with the green chilies, Harry got back to business.

"Prague, Pamplona and Rio," he recited with just a hint of hoarseness. "We've suspected all along that our man is triangulating his shipments."

"Triangulating them?"

"Sending them through second and third countries, where they're rebundled with other products like coffee or bat guano, then smuggled into the States."

"Why in the world would someone bundle uranium with bat guano and...? Oh! To disguise the scent of the metal containers and get them past the Customs dogs, right?"

"You got it in one." He leaned forward, all business now. "Can you remember any of the words on the cards?"

"On two of them. I didn't see the one from Prague. My friend Elise described it to me, though."

"Okay, start with Rio. Give me what you can remember."

"I can give it to you exactly." She wrinkled her brow. "'Hi to my favorite aunt. I've been dancing in the streets for the past four days. Wish you were here.'"

Harry stared at her in blank astonishment. "You can recall it word for word?"

"Sure."

"How?" he shot back. "With the thousands of pieces of mail you handle every day, how in the hell can you remember one postcard?"

"Because I handle thousands of pieces of mail every day," she explained patiently. "The white envelopes and brown flats—the paper-wrapped magazines and manila envelopes—all blur together. Not that many postcards come through, though, and when they do, they catch our attention immediately."

She decided not to add that the really interesting postcards got passed from employee to employee. The male workers particularly enjoyed the topless beach scenes that American tourists loved to send back to their relatives. Some cards went well beyond topless and tipped into outright obscenity. Those they were required to turn into the postal inspectors. Sheryl had long ago ceased being surprised at what people stuck stamps on and dropped in a mailbox.

Harry had her repeat the message. He copied the few sentences in his pad, then studied their content.

"I don't think this is Carnival season. I'm sure that happens right before Lent in Rio, just as it does in New Orleans."

He made another note to himself to check the dates of Rio's famous festival. Sheryl was sitting so close she could make out every stroke. His handwriting mirrored his personality, she decided. Bold. Aggressive. Impatient.

"Maybe the four days has some significance," she suggested.

"It probably does." He frowned down at his notes. "I don't know what yet, though."

"Do you want to know about the picture on the front side?" she asked after a moment.

"Later. Let's finish the back first. What else do you remember about it?"

"What do you want to start with? The handwriting? The color of ink? The stamp? The cancellation mark?"

He sat back, his eyes gleaming. He looked like a man who'd just hit a superjackpot.

"Start wherever you want."

They worked their way right through sour cream enchiladas, smoked charro beans, rice and sopapillas dripping with honey. The mariachi band came to their table and left again, richer by the generous tip Harry passed them. The tables around them emptied, refilled. They were still working the Rio postcard when Harry's phone beeped.

"MacMillan." He listened for a moment, his brow creasing. "Right. I'm on my way."

Snapping the phone shut, he rose to pull out Sheryl's chair. "I'm sorry. Inga Gunderson's lawyer just showed up and wants to see his client. We'll have to go over the rest of the cards tomorrow. I'll call you to set up a time."

A small, unexpected dart of pleasure rippled through Sheryl at the thought of continuing this discussion with Marshal MacMillan. Shrugging, she chalked it up to the fact that she still had something worthwhile to contribute to his investigation.

She drove out of the parking lot a few moments later, thinking that she'd better reschedule the last-minute layette shopping spree she and Elise had planned for tomorrow night. As determined as Harry was to extract every last bit of information from her, they might have to work late.

She couldn't know that he would walk into the post office just after nine the next morning and reschedule her entire life.

Chapter 4

"I'm sorry, sir," Sheryl repeated for the third time. "I can't hand out a DHS check over the counter. Even if I could, I wouldn't give you a check addressed to someone else."

The runny-eyed scarecrow on the other side of the counter lifted an arm and swiped it across his nose. His hand shook so badly that the tattoos decorating the inside of his wrist were a blur of red and blue.

"That's my old lady's welfare check," he whined. "I gotta have it. I want it."

Yeah, right, Sheryl thought. What he wanted was another fix, courtesy of the Department of Human Services. She wondered how many other women this creep had bullied or beaten out of their food and rent money over the years to feed his drug habit.

"I can't give it to you," she repeated.

"My old lady's moved, I'm tellin' ya, and she didn't get her check this month. She sent me in to pick it up."

"I'm sure someone explained to her that the post office can't forward a DHS check. We're required by regulations to deliver it to the address where she physically resides or send it back."

"Send it back? Why, dammit?"

The angry explosion turned the heads of the other customers who'd come in with the first rush of the morning. In the booth next to Sheryl's, Elise glanced up sharply from the stamps she was dealing out.

Holding on to her patience with both hands, Sheryl tried again. "We have to send the checks back to DHS because a few people abused the system by moving constantly and collecting checks from several different counties at once. Now everyone has to pay the price for their fraud."

The lank-haired junkie fixed her with a malevolent glare. "Yeah, well, I don't give a rat's ass about them other people. I just want my old lady's money. You'd better give it to me, bitch, or I'm gonna—"

"You're going to what?"

At the dangerous drawl, both Sheryl and her unpleasant customer jerked around.

The sight of Harry MacMillan's broad-shouldered form sent relief pinging through her. Relief and something else, something far too close to excitement for Sheryl's peace of mind. Swallowing, she ascribed the sudden flutter in her stomach to the fact that the marshal looked particularly intimidating this morning.

As he had yesterday, he wore jeans and a well-tailored sport coat, this one a soft, lightweight, blue broadcloth. As it had yesterday, his jacket strained at the seams of his wide shoulders. Adding to his overall physical presence, his jaw had a hard edge that sent off its own silent warning. The gold in his eyes glinted hard and cold.

Sheryl could handle nasty characters like the one standing in front of her at this moment. She'd done it many times. But that didn't stop her from enjoying the pasty look that came over the druggie's face when he took in Harry's size and stance.

"Nah, no problem," he replied to Harry, but his mouth pinched when he turned back to Sheryl. "Me 'n' my old lady need that money."

"Tell her to contact DHS," She instructed once again. "They'll issue an emergency payment if necessary."

His thin, ravaged face contorted with fury and a need she could only begin to guess at. "I wouldn't be here if it wasn't necessary, you stupid—"

He broke off, slinging a sideways look at Harry.

The marshal jerked his head toward the lobby doors. "You'd better leave, pal. Now."

The watery eyes flared with reckless bravado. "You gonna make me, *pal?*"

"If I have to."

Like waves eddying around a rock, the other customers in the post office backed away from the two men. A tight, taut silence gripped the area. Sheryl's knee inched toward the silent alarm button just under her counter.

The thin, pinch-faced junkie broke the shimmering tension just before she exerted enough pressure to set off the alarm. With another spiteful glance at Sheryl, he pushed past Harry and shouldered open the glass door. A collective murmur of relief rose from the other customers as the door thumped shut behind him.

Harry didn't relax his vigilance until the departing figure had stalked to a battered motorcycle, threw a leg over the seat, jumped on the starter and roared out of the parking lot.

"Nice guy," one of the women in line murmured.

"Wonder what his problem was?" another groused.

"Do you get many customers like that?" Harry inquired, moving to Sheryl's station.

No one objected to the fact that he cut ahead of them in line, she noticed.

"Not many. What are you doing here? I thought you were going to call and set up a time for us to meet?"

"I decided to come in person, instead. Can you get someone to cover for you here? I need to talk to you privately."

"Yes, of course. Wait for me in the lobby and I'll let you in through that door to the back area."

With a nod to the other customers, Harry turned away. Elise demanded an explanation the moment the glass doors swung shut behind him.

"Who *is* that?"

"He's—"

Sheryl caught herself just in time. Harry had told her not to discuss the case with anyone other than her supervisor. She hadn't, although the restriction had resulted in another uncomfortable phone conversation with Brian after she'd driven home from El Pinto.

"He's an acquaintance," she finished lamely, if truthfully.

"Since when?"

"Since last night."

Elise's dark-red brows pulled together in a troubled frown. "Does Brian know about this new acquaintance of yours?"

"There's nothing to know." With an apologetic smile at the lined-up customers, Sheryl plopped a Closed sign in front of her station. "I'll send Peggy up to cover the counter with you."

She found the petite brunette on the outside loading dock, pulling in long, contented drags of cigarette smoke mixed with diesel fumes from the mail truck parked next to the ramp.

"I know you're on break, but something's come up. Can you cover for me out front for a few minutes?"

"Sure." Peggy took another pull, then stubbed out her cigarette in the tub of sand the irreverent carriers always referred to as the butt box. Carefully, she tucked the half-smoked cigarette into the pocket of her uniform shirt.

"I have to conserve every puff. I promised myself I'd only smoke a half a pack today."

"I thought you decided to quit completely."

"I did! I will! After this pack. Maybe." Smiling ruefully at Sheryl's grin, she strolled back into the station. "How long do you think you'll be? I'm supposed to help Pat with the vault inventory this morning."

"Not long," Sheryl assured her. "I just need to set up an appointment."

* * *

Contrary to her expectations, she soon discovered that Harry hadn't driven to the Monzano station to make an appointment.

She stared at him, dumbfounded, while he calmly informed her and her supervisor that Albuquerque's postmaster had agreed to assign Miss Hancock to the special fugitive apprehension task force that Harry headed.

"Me?"

Sheryl's startled squeak echoed off the walls of the stationmaster's little-used private office.

"You," he confirmed, pulling a folded document out of his coat pocket. "This authorizes an indefinite detail, effective immediately."

"May I see that?" her supervisor asked.

"Of course."

Pat Martinez stuck her pencil into her upswept jet-black hair and skimmed the brief communiqué he handed her.

"Well, it looks like you're on temporary duty, Sheryl."

"Hey, hang on here," she protested. "I'm not sure I want to be assigned to a fugitive apprehension task force, indefinitely or otherwise. Before I agree to anything like this, I want to know what's required of me."

"Basically, I want your exclusive time and attention for as long it takes to extract every bit of information I can about those postcards."

"Exclusive time and attention? You mean, like all day?"

"And all night, if necessary."

Sheryl gaped at him. "You're kidding, right?"

He didn't crack so much as a hint of a smile. "No, Miss Hancock, I'm not. My team's been at it pretty much around the clock since we tracked Inga Gunderson to Albuquerque. I won't ask that you put in twenty-four hours at a stretch, of course, but I will ask that you work with me as long as necessary and as hard as possible."

"Look, I don't mind working with you, but we're shorthanded here. The box clerk is on vacation and Elise could go out on maternity leave at any moment."

"So the postmaster indicated." Calmly, Harry nodded to the document held by Sheryl's supervisor. "We took that into consideration."

"The postmaster is sending a temp to cover your absence," Pat explained. "If Elise goes out, he'll cover that, too." Her eyes lifted to Harry. "You're thorough, MacMillan."

"I learned my lesson after the fiasco with the warrant," he admitted. "This time, I made sure we dotted every i and crossed every t."

Sheryl wasn't sure she liked being lumped in with the i's and t's, but she let it pass. Now that she'd recovered from her initial surprise, she didn't object to the detail. She just didn't care for Harry's high-handed way of arranging it.

As if realizing that he needed to mend some bridges with his new detailee, the marshal gave her a smile that tried for apologetic but fell a few degrees short. Sheryl suspected that MacMillan rarely apologized for anything.

"I didn't have time to coordinate this with you and Ms. Martinez beforehand. My partner and I were up most of the night running air routes that service Prague, Pamplona and Rio through the computers. We're convinced our man is bringing in a shipment soon, and we're not going to let it or him slip through our fingers. We've got to break the code that was on those postcards, and to do that we need your help, Sheryl."

Put like that, how could she refuse?

"Well, if you're sure someone's coming out here to cover for me…"

"The postmaster assured me that wasn't a problem."

Sheryl looked to Pat, who nodded. "We'll manage until the temp gets here. Go close down your station."

Still a little bemused by her sudden transition from postal clerk to task force augmentee, Sheryl headed for the front. Naturally, her curious co-workers peppered her with questions.

"What's going on, Sher?" Elise wanted to know. "Why are you closing out?"

Peggy grinned wickedly over the divider separating the stations. "And who's the long, tall stud with the mustache? Tell us all, girl."

"I can't right now. I'll tell you about it later."

When she could, Sheryl amended silently, hitting a sequence of keystrokes to tally her counter transactions. The printer stuttered out a report for her abridged workday. Another quick sequence shut down the computer.

Her hand resting on her mounded tummy, Elise waited for the next customer. "Where are you going now?"

That much at least Sheryl could reveal. "Downtown. The postmaster has assigned me to a special detail."

"With the stud? No kidding?" Peggy waggled her brows. "How do I go about getting assigned to this detail?"

"By stopping by to check on little old ladies on your way home from work."

"Huh?"

"I'll tell you about it later," Sheryl repeated.

With swift efficiency, she ejected her disk from her terminal and removed her cash drawer. After stacking her stock of stamps on top of the drawer, she carried the lot to the vault. A quick inventory tallied her cash receipts with the money orders, stamps and supplies she'd sold so far this morning. She scribbled her name across the report, then left it for the T-6 clerk who had the unenviable task of reconciling all the counter clerks' reports with the master printout produced at the end of each day. That done, she hurried back to her counter to retrieve her purse and extract a promise from Elise.

"Brian's supposed to pick me up at eleven-thirty. He wanted to show me a house during lunch that he's going to list. He needs a woman's opinion about the renovations that might be necessary to the kitchen. Would you go with him? Please? You know how he always raves about what you did with your kitchen."

Brian wasn't the only one who raved about the miracles Elise had performed with the small fixer-upper he'd found for her after her divorce. With two kids to house and a third about to make an appearance, she'd taken wallpapering and sheet curtains to a higher plane of art. She'd also turned a dilapidated kitchen into a marvel of bleached cabinets, hand-decorated tiles and artfully disguised pipes.

"I'll be happy to go with him, but…"

"Thanks! Tell him I'll call him tonight."

Sheryl left Elise with a frown still creasing her forehead and hurried toward the back. Now that she'd gotten used to the idea, she had to admit the prospect of taking part in a criminal investigation sent a little thrill of excitement through her. The Wanted posters tacked to the bulletin board in the outer lobby and the occasional creeps who came into the post office, like the one this morning, were the closest she'd come to the dark, seamy side of life. Besides, she was only doing her civic duty by helping Harry piece together the puzzle of the postcards.

Which didn't explain the way her pulse seemed to stutter with that strange, inexplicable excitement when she saw the marshal. Hands shoved into his pockets, ankles crossed, he lounged against one of the carriers' sorting desks as though he had nothing else in the world more important to do than wait for her. The pose didn't fit his character, she now knew. Harry MacMillan was anything but patient. She'd just met him yesterday— fallen into his arms, more correctly—and now he'd pulled her off her job to work on his team.

At the sound of her footsteps, he glanced up, and Sheryl's excitement took on a deeper, keener edge. His toffee-colored eyes swept her with the same intent scrutiny that had raised goose bumps on her skin yesterday. Suddenly self-conscious, she glanced down at her pin-striped shirt with its neat little cross tab tie and her navy shorts.

"Should I change out of my uniform?"

His gaze skimmed from her nose to her knees and back again. "You're fine."

She was a whole lot better than fine, Harry thought as he followed her to the exit. He'd never paid much attention to postal uniforms, but Sheryl Hancock filled hers out nicely. Very nicely.

Her pin-striped shirt with its little red tab was innocuous enough, but the long, curving stretch of leg displayed by those navy shorts pushed his simple observation into swift, gut-level male appreciation. It also put a knot in his belly that didn't belong there right now.

Frowning, Harry gave himself a mental shake. He'd better keep his mind focused on the information Sheryl could supply, not on her tanned legs or the seductive swing of her hips. And he'd darn well better remember why he'd yanked her from her workplace and put her on his team. She held the key to those damned postcards. He felt it with every instinct he possessed. He wasn't going to rest until he'd pulled every scrap of information out of this woman.

Despite his stern reminder that his business with Sheryl was just that, business, his pulse tripped at the thought of the hours ahead. On the advice of her lawyer, Inga Gunderson flatly refused to talk to the investigators. Harry and Ev had spent several frustrating hours with the woman last night. Finally, they'd left her stewing in her own venom. The clerk of the court had assured them that she wouldn't get a bail hearing until late tomorrow, if then, given the overloaded court docket.

Earlier this morning, Ev had left to drive up to the

labs at Los Alamos to talk to one of the government's foremost experts on the use and physical properties of depleted uranium. The New Mexico state trooper assigned to the task force was now out at the local FAA office, compiling a list of secondary airstrips within a hundred-mile radius. The Customs agent working with them on an as-needed basis had returned to his office to cull through foreign flight schedules. For the next few hours at least, Harry would have the task force headquarters—and Sheryl—to himself.

He intended to make good use of that time.

"Why don't I drive, since my vehicle is cleared for the secure parking at the Chavez Federal Building? We can come back for your car later."

"Okay. Just let me open my windows a bit to keep from baking the seats."

A moment later, Sheryl buckled herself into the blast furnace heat of the tan sedan. "So you're operating out of the downtown courthouse?"

"We've set up task force headquarters in the U.S. Marshals' offices."

Task force headquarters!

A vague image formed in her mind of a busy, high-tech command post, complete with wall-sized screen satellite maps displaying all kinds of vital information, humming computer terminals, beeping phones and a team of dedicated, intense professionals. The idea of becoming a part, however briefly, of the effort kindled a sense of adventure.

Reality came crashing down on her the moment she stepped inside the third-floor conference room in the multistory federal building in the heart of the city. Hand-scribbled paper charts decorated the nondescript tan walls. Foam coffee cups and cardboard boxes of records littered the long conference table. Wires from the phones clustered in the center of the table snaked around the cups and over the boxes like gray streamers. A faint, stale odor drifted from the crushed pizza cartons that had been stuffed into metal wastebaskets in a corner. Sheryl looked around, gulping.

"This is it? Your headquarters?"

"This is it." Harry shrugged off the clutter with the same ease he shrugged out of his jacket. "Make yourself comfortable."

She might have been able to do just that if her gaze hadn't snagged on the blue steel gun butt nestled against his left side. Even holstered, the weapon looked ugly and far too dangerous for her peace of mind.

Harry tossed his jacket over a chair back and turned, catching her wary expression. "Don't worry. I know how to use it."

Somehow, that didn't reassure her.

"I don't like guns," she admitted, dropping her shoulder bag into a chair. "They make me nervous. Very nervous."

Calmly, he rolled up the cuffs of his white cotton shirt. "They make me nervous, too. Especially when they're loaded with uranium-tipped bullets. Ready to get to work?"

After that unsubtle reminder of the reason she was here, Sheryl could hardly say no. Pulling out one of the chairs, she rolled up to the table.

"I'm ready."

"We pretty well took apart the postcard from Rio last night. Let's start with the one from Pamplona today. We'll reverse the process and work the front side first. Can you describe the scene?"

She shot him an amused glance.

"Of course you can," he answered himself. "You talk, I'll listen."

Summoning up a mental image of the card, Sheryl painted a vivid word picture that included a narrow, cobbled street lined with two-story stone houses. Geranium-filled window boxes. White-shirted young men racing between the buildings, looking over their shoulders at the herd of black bulls just visible at a bend in the street.

Harry copied down every word, so intent on searching for similarities with the card from Rio that it was some time before he noticed the subtle difference in Sheryl's voice. It sounded softer, he realized in surprise, almost dreamy. He glanced up to find her staring at the wall, her mouth curving slightly. She'd gotten lost somewhere on a high, sunny plain in Spain's Basque province.

Harry got a little lost himself just looking at her. The faint trace of freckles across the bridge of her nose fascinated him, as did the mass of tawny hair tumbling down her back. She'd pulled the hair at her temples back and caught it in one of those plastic clips with long, dangerous-looking teeth. His hand itched to spring the clip free, to let those curls take on a life of their own.

"There was a cathedral in the background," she murmured, drawing his attention away from the curve of her cheek. "An old Gothic cathedral complete with flying buttresses and a huge rose-colored window in the south transept. One of man's finest monuments to God."

Sighing, she shifted in her seat and caught Harry staring at her. "I've read a little bit about medieval Gothic cathedrals," she confessed with an embarrassed shrug. "Some people consider them the architectural wonders of the modern world."

"Have you ever been inside one?"

"No. Have you?"

He nodded. "Notre Dame."

"In Paris?"

Her breathless awe made Harry bite back a grin. He'd visited the majestic structure on a wet, dreary spring day. All he could recall were impenetrable shadows, cold dampness and thousands of votive candles flickering in the darkness. Of course, he was a marine gunny sergeant on leave at the time, and far more interested in the *filles de joie* working the broad embankments along the Seine than in the gray stone cathedral

"Maybe your sort-of fiancé will spring for a trip to Paris for a honeymoon," he commented casually.

He saw at once that he'd said the wrong thing. The soft, faraway look disappeared from her green eyes. She sat up, a tiny frown creasing her brow.

"Brian isn't interested in traveling, any more than I am. We prefer to save our money for something more practical, like a house or a new car or the kids' college education."

Without warning, a thought rifled through Harry's mind. If he wanted to stake his claim to a woman like this one, he'd whisk her off to a deserted island, peel off her clothes and make love to her a dozen times a day before either of them started thinking about a house and a new car and the kids' college education.

His belly clenched at the image of Sheryl sprawled in the surf, her tanned body offered up to the sun like a pagan sacrifice. Her arms reached for him. Her eyes…

Dammit!

A quick shake of his head banished the crashing surf. He had to remember why he was here. And that Sheryl was spoken for…almost. Pushing aside her vague relationship with the jerk who made appointments instead of dates, he brought them both back to the matter at hand.

"Let's talk about the message on the back."

She blinked at his brusque instruction, but complied willingly enough.

"As best I recall, it was short and sweet. 'Hi, Auntie. I've spent two great…'" She paused, chewing on her lower lip. "No, it was three. 'I've spent three great days keeping a half step ahead of the bulls. See you soon, Paul.'"

"Run it through your mind again," Harry ordered. "Close your eyes. See the words. Picture the—"

One of the phones on the table shrilled. He grabbed the receiver, listened for a few minutes and hung up with a promise to call back later.

"Close your eyes, Sheryl."

Obediently, she blanked out the chart-strewn walls.

"Visualize the words. Follow every curl of every letter. Describe them to me."

Like a dutiful disciple of a master mesmerizer, she let Harry's deep, slow voice lull her into a state of near somnolence. Slowly, lines of dark swirls began to take shape.

She didn't even notice when morning faded into afternoon, or when the uninspiring conference room began to take on an aura of a real live operations center. She did note that the phones rang constantly, and that a seemingly steady stream of people popped in to talk to Harry or pass information.

Sometime around the middle of the afternoon, the short, stocky Everett Sloan returned from Los Alamos Laboratories. Sheryl soon discovered that, unlike Harry, he was assigned to the Albuquerque office of the U.S. Marshals and had been tapped as the local coordinator for the task force. Shedding his wrinkled suit jacket, Ev informed his temporary partner that he'd collected more information than he'd ever wanted to know about the properties and characteristics of the heavy metal known as U-235.

A short time later, a slender, striking brunette in the brown shirt, gray pants and Smoky the Bear hat of a New Mexico state trooper joined the group. After brief introductions, Fay Chandler tossed her hat on the table and unrolled a huge aerial map showing every airstrip, paved or otherwise, within a hundred-mile radius. The three-letter designation code for each strip had been highlighted in yellow. If their suspect intended to bring his contraband in someplace other than Albuquerque International, Fay would coordinate the local response team.

In the midst of all this activity, Harry somehow remained focused on Sheryl and the postcards. After hours of work, he reduced the sheets of information he'd pulled from her to a few key words and phrases. He repeated them now in an almost singsong mantra.

"Rio…Carnival…April…four."

Sheryl picked up the chorus. "Pamplona…bulls… July… three."

"Prague…Wenceslas Square…September…two."

MacMillan stared at the words, as though the sheer intensity of his scrutiny would solve the riddle they represented. "I know there's a pattern in there somewhere. A reverse order of numbers or letters or something!"

"Maybe the computers will find it." Ev Sloan slid his thumbs under his flashy red-and-yellow Bugs Bunny suspenders to hitch up his pants. "I'll go down to the data center and plug the key words in. The airstrip designation codes, too. Be back in a flash with the trash."

Harry caught Sheryl's smile and put a more practical spin on Ev's blithe remark. "You'll think it's trash, too, when you see the endless combinations the computers will kick out. It'll take us the rest of the evening, if not the night, to go over them."

Sheryl's smile fizzled. Good grief! He hadn't been kidding about working day and night. She snuck a peek at the clock on the wall. It was after five. They'd worked right through lunch. The Diet Pepsis and bags of Krispy Korn Kurls Harry had procured from the vending machines down the hall had long since disappeared. Practical considerations such as real food and a cool shower and retrieving her car from the post office parking lot crept into Sheryl's mind.

As if to echo her thoughts, a loud, rolling growl issued from her tummy.

"I'm a creature of habit," she offered apologetically when Harry glanced her way. "I tend to crave food… real food…a couple of times a day."

He speared a look at the clock, then reached for the jacket he'd tossed over a chair back hours ago. "Sorry. I didn't intend to starve you. There's a decent Italian sub shop across the street. Ev, Fay, you two up for another round of green peppers and sausage?"

Ev shook his head. "I want to get the computers rolling. Bring me back a garlic sausage special."

"I'll pass, too," Fay put in. "My youngest has a T-ball game at six-thirty and I swore on his stack of Goosebumps that I'd make this one. I'll come back here after the game's over, Harry."

MacMillan shrugged into his jacket. "You've been at this hard for the past three days and nights. Relax and enjoy the game."

Laughing, Fay rerolled her aeronautical maps. "Your single status is showing, Marshal. Anyone with kids would know better than to advise a parent to relax at a T-ball game."

"I stand corrected."

So he was single. Without knowing why she did so, Sheryl tucked that bit of information away for future reference. She'd noticed that he didn't wear a wedding ring. A lot of men didn't, of course, but the confirmation that the marshal was neither married nor a parent added a new dimension to the man…and triggered a whole new set of questions in her mind. Was he divorced? Currently involved with someone? Seeing someone who didn't mind the fact that he spent almost all his time away from home, chasing fugitives?

Sheryl shook off her intense curiosity about the marshal with something of an effort. His personal life had nothing to do with her, she reminded herself, or with her part in his investigation. She shifted her attention to Fay, who winked and settled her hat on her sleek, dark hair.

"Some people think that high-speed chases in pursuit of fleeing suspects and cement-footed drunks are tough, but I'm here to tell you that keeping up with my four rug-rats takes a whole lot more stamina."

"I don't have any rug-rats at home, but I can imag—" Sheryl stopped abruptly, her eyes widening. "Oh, no! I do!"

"If you're referring to the obnoxious rodent you insisted on taking home with you," Harry drawled, "I can't think of a more perfect description."

She grabbed her purse, trying not to think of the damage the shih tzu might have done to her dining-room chairs and pale-mauve carpet during his long incarceration.

"I have to swing by the post office to get my car, then go home to let Button out," she said worriedly.

"Good enough. We can grab some dinner on the way."

The thought of sharing another meal with Harry sent a tingle of anticipation down Sheryl's spine…

followed by an instant rush of guilt. Belatedly, she realized that she hadn't even thought of Brian since early morning. The marshal's forceful personality and fierce determination to bring Richard Johnson-Paul Gunderson to justice had swept her right into the stream of the investigation, to the exclusion of all else.

"I'd better pass on dinner, too," she said. "I'll grab a sandwich at home."

And call Brian.

The task force leader conceded the point with a small shrug. "Whatever works."

Just as well, Harry thought as he waited beside Sheryl for the elevator to the underground parking. This manhunt had consumed him for almost a year, yet today he'd had to fight to stay focused on the information his newest team member was providing. Harry knew damn well that Sheryl didn't have any idea of the way his muscles had clenched every time she'd leaned over to check his notes. Or the havoc she'd caused to his concentration whenever she'd stretched out those long, tanned legs. After almost eight hours of breathing her scent and registering every nuance in her voice and body language, Harry figured he'd better put some distance between them. He needed to regain his sharp-edged sense of purpose, which was proving more difficult than he would have imagined around Sheryl.

They turned into the Monzano station well after six. To the east, the jagged Sandia Mountains were beginning to take on the watermelon-pink hue that the Spaniards had named them for. To the west, the sun blazed a fiery gold above the five volcanoes that rose from the lava fields like stubby sentinels.

The station's front parking lot had long since emptied, and a high, sliding gate blocked the entrance to the fenced-in rear lot. Rows of white Jeeps with the postal service's distinctive red-and-blue markings filled the back parking area. Sheryl spied her ice-blue Camry at the far end of the lot.

"You can let me out here," she told Harry. "I have a key card to activate the gate. I'll see you back at the courthouse in an hour or so."

"I'll wait here until you drive out."

She didn't argue. Although the station was located in a quiet, residential neighborhood, it took in large amounts of cash every day. They'd never had a robbery at the Manzano station, but postal bulletins regularly warned employees to stay alert when coming in early or leaving late. After keying the gate, Sheryl waited while the metal wheels rattled and bumped across the concrete. Her footsteps made little sucking noises as she crossed asphalt still soft from the scorching afternoon sun.

She was almost to her car when she heard a clink behind her. It sounded as though someone or something had bumped into a parked Jeep. Sheryl glanced over her shoulder. Nothing moved except the elongated shadow that floated at an angle behind her. Frowning, she dug in her purse for her keys and wound through the last row of vehicles at a brisk pace. Relief rippled through her as she approached her trusty little Camry. When she got her first full look at the car, relief melted into instant dismay. The vehicle sat low to the ground. Too low. Keys in hand, Sheryl stood staring at its board-flat tires.

Slowly, she moved closer and bent to examine the front tire. It hadn't just gone flat, she saw with a sudden, hollow sensation. It had been slashed. She was still poking at the gaping wounds in the rubber with her finger when another sound cut through the stillness like a knife.

Her heart leaping into her throat, Sheryl spun around. The slanting rays of the sun hit her full in the face…and blurred the dark silhouette of the figure looming over her.

Chapter 5

"What the hell…?"

Sheryl recognized Harry's broad-shouldered form at almost the same moment his voice penetrated her sudden, paralyzing fear.

Without stopping to think, without taking a breath, she flowed toward him. She didn't expect him to curl an arm around her and draw her hard against his body, but she certainly didn't protest when he did. She closed her eyes, taking shameless comfort in his presence. It was a moment before she managed to murmur a shaky explanation.

"Someone slashed my tires."

"So I see," he rasped, his voice low and tight above her head. "I got antsy about letting you walk back here alone. Looks like I had reason to."

His muscles twisting like steel under her cheek, he turned to survey the parking lot and the wire fence surrounding it.

"Not a security camera in sight," he muttered in disgust.

Slowly, Sheryl disengaged from his hold. She was still shaken enough to miss the security of his arms, but not so much that she didn't realize the feel of his body pressed against hers wasn't helping her regain her equilibrium. Swallowing, she tried to steady her nerves while he completed a scowling survey of the area.

The vista on the other side of the fence didn't afford him any more satisfaction than the lack of outside cameras in the parking lot. A tumbleweed-strewn field cut by a jagged arroyo separated the station from the residential area. The landscape shimmered with a silvery beauty that only someone used to New Mexico's serene, natural emptiness could appreciate. At this moment, all Sheryl could think of was how easily someone could have crossed the emptiness and scaled the wire link fence.

Echoing her thoughts, Harry scanned the residences in the distance and shook his head. "Those houses are too far away for anyone to spot a fence climber. The post office should have better security."

"That's assuming whoever cut my tires climbed the fence. He could've just walked into the lot. With all the carriers coming and going, we don't keep the gates locked during the day."

"I know."

Belatedly, she remembered that Harry had driven in and out of those open gates with her several times. She wasn't thinking clearly, she realized.

He went down on one knee to examine the tires. "We're also assuming that an outsider caused this damage."

A new series of shocks eddied through Sheryl. "You can't think anyone at the post office would cut my tires like that."

He rose, dusting his hands. "Why not?"

"They're my friends as well as my co-workers!"

"All of them?"

"Well…"

She could name one carrier whose coarse, barroom style of humor had resulted in a couple of private and very heated discussions about what was considered acceptable language in the workplace. Then there was that temporary Christmas clerk who'd pestered her for dates long after she and Brian started seeing each other. Neither of those men had ever shown any animosity toward her, however. Certainly not the kind of animosity that would lead to something like this.

"Yes," she finished. "All of them."

Harry lifted a skeptical brow but didn't argue. "Well, I suspect you can't say the same about all of your customers."

"No." She shuddered, thinking of the thin, hostile doper who'd confronted her across the counter this morning. "I can't."

"That's why I followed you into the parking lot. I got to thinking about the crackhead who'd threatened you." He hesitated, then continued slowly. "I also got to thinking about the fact that right now you're my only link to Inga Gunderson's nephew."

Sheryl stared up at him in confusion. "What could that have to do with my slashed tires?"

"Maybe nothing," he answered, his face tight. "Maybe everything."

Before she could make any sense of that, he pulled out his phone. "Let's get the police out here to check the area before I call Ev."

Her mind whirling, Sheryl listened while he contacted the Albuquerque police and asked them to send a patrol car to the Monzano station right away. A moment later, he made a short, succinct call to his partner.

"Find out if the Gunderson woman contacted anyone other than her lawyer, or if she sent out any messages, written or otherwise. I want every second of her time accounted for since we brought her in yesterday afternoon."

Yesterday afternoon? Sheryl shook her head in disbelief. Was it only yesterday afternoon that she'd driven to Inga Gunderson's house, worried about the woman's well-being? Just a little more than twenty-four hours since she'd practically fallen into Harry MacMillan's arms? It seemed longer. A whole lot longer!

No wonder, considering all that had happened in those hours. She'd stood Brian up not once but twice. She'd gained a thoroughly obnoxious houseguest. She'd transitioned from postal clerk to task force augmentee without so much as five minutes' notice. And she'd just lost four tires that she'd planned to squeeze another thousand miles out of, despite the fact that the tread had pretty well disappeared. She was wondering if her insurance would cover the cost of replacements when she caught the tail end of Harry's conversation.

"Finish up at Miss Hancock's apartment. I'll call you when I get through." He snapped the phone shut.

"Finish up what at my apartment?"

"I'm going to follow you home after we get done here. I want to check your locks."

"Check my locks? Why?"

"Just in case the person who did this also knows where you live."

"Oh."

Harry's eyes narrowed at the sudden catch in her voice. Sliding the phone into his pocket, he nodded toward the loading dock.

"Let's wait over there, out of the heat."

Sheryl trailed beside him, but she didn't need the shade offered by the overhanging roof to cut the effects of the sun. The idea that the person responsible for the damage to her car might also know her home address had cooled her considerably. Harry's carefully neutral expression only added to that chill.

"I'm not trying to scare you," he said evenly, "but this wasn't a random act. The perpetrator didn't vandalize any of the other vehicles. Only yours."

"I noticed that."

"He could have done it out of spite." He slanted her a careful look. "Or he might have been trying to disable your car so you couldn't drive off when you came back to the post office…although there are certainly less obvious ways of doing that."

"For someone who isn't trying to scare me, you're doing a darn good job of it!"

"Sorry."

Blowing out a long breath, he tried to recover the ground he'd just lost.

"Look, all cops are suspicious by nature, and most of us are downright paranoid. I'm reaching here, really reaching, to even imagine a connection between this incident and the fact that Inga Gunderson knows you're providing us information about her postcards."

"I hope so!"

The near panic in her voice brought his brows down in a quick frown. Cursing under his breath, he back-pedaled even more.

"I'll wait to see if the police can lift any prints from the car before I speculate any further. In the meantime, try to think of anyone who might hold a grudge against you or want to get even over something."

"Other than the creep this morning, I can't think of anyone. I lead a pretty quiet life aside from my work."

"That doesn't say a lot for your fiancé," MacMillan offered as an aside. "Correction, sort-of fiancé."

A tinge of heat took some of the chill from Sheryl's cheeks. "Brian and I are very comfortable together."

His brow went up. "That says even less."

"Yes, well, not everyone wants to go chasing all over the world after bad guys, Marshal. Some of us prefer a more settled kind of life, not to mention unslashed tires."

"We'll get the tires fixed and put a—"

He broke off, his head lifting at the sound of a siren in the distance. It drew closer, the wail undulating through the evening stillness. Sheryl gave a little breath of relief.

"They got here fast."

Harry pushed away from the dock. "That's one of the benefits of having a representative from the Albuquerque Police Department on the task force. Come on, let's go direct them to the crime scene."

Hearing her trusty little Camry described as a "crime scene" didn't exactly soothe the victim's ragged nerves. She trailed after MacMillan, sincerely wishing Mrs. Inga Gunderson had never brought her melt-in-your-mouth cookies and yappy little dog into the Monzano Street station.

The reminder that the yappy little dog had no doubt spent the day demolishing Sheryl's apartment didn't particularly help matters, either.

By the time the police finished their investigation of the scene and a twenty-four-hour roadside service had replaced the Camry's tires, the spectacular light show that constituted a New Mexico sunset had begun. The entire western horizon blazed with color. Streaks of pink and turquoise layered into vibrant reds and velvet purples. The sun hovered like a shimmering gold fireball just above the Rio Grande. As Sheryl drove up the sloping rise toward her east-side apartment with Harry following close behind, the city lights twinkled like earthbound stars in her rearview mirror.

The serenity and beauty of the descending night helped loosen the tight knot of tension at the back of her neck. The police hadn't found anything that would identify the slasher. No prints, no footprints, no personal item conveniently dropped at the scene as so often occurred in movies and detective novels. The police had promised to canvas the houses that backed onto the fields around the station, but didn't hold out any more hope than Harry had that someone might have witnessed the vandalism. Tomorrow, they would interview Sheryl's co-workers. Rumors would speed like runaway roadrunners around the post office with this incident coming on top of her sudden detail. Elise must be wondering what in the world her friend had gotten herself into.

She'd call her tonight, Sheryl decided. And Brian. Despite the marshal's orders, she had to tell them something. They were her best friends.

When she caught her train of thought, Sheryl's hands tightened on the steering wheel. When had she started thinking of Brian as a friend, not a lover, for goodness' sake? And why did Harry's little editorial comments about their relationship raise her hackles?

Frowning, she waited for the easy slide of comfort that always accompanied any reminder of Brian and their future together. It came, but it brought along with it another traitorous thought. Was comfort really what she wanted in a marriage?

Oh, great! As if escaped fugitives, smuggled uranium and slashed tires weren't enough, Sheryl had to pick now of all times to question a relationship that she'd happily taken for granted until this minute.

The events of the past two days had rattled her, she decided. Both her home and her work schedule had been thrown off-kilter, as had the comfortable routine she and Brian had fallen into. As soon as she finished this detail and Harry MacMillan went chasing after his fugitive, her life would return to its normal, regular pace.

Sheryl pulled into her assigned parking slot, wondering why in the world the prospect didn't cheer her as much as it should have. A car door slammed in the area reserved for visitor parking, then Harry appeared beside the Camry. As he had before, he opened Sheryl's door and reached down a hand to help her out.

Oddly reluctant, she put her hand in his. The small electrical jolt that raced from her palm to her wrist to her elbow did *not* help resolve the confusion that welled in her mind. With a distinct lack of graciousness for the small courtesy, Sheryl yanked her hand free and led the way through the two-story adobe buildings.

While she fumbled through the keys for the one to her front door, Harry swept an appreciative eye around the tiled courtyard shared by the eight apartments in her cluster. Soft light from strategically placed luminaria bathed the little bubbling fountain and wooden benches carved with New Mexico's zia symbol. Clay pots spilled a profusion of flowers that hadn't yet folded their petals for the night. Their fragrance hung on the descending dusk like a gauzy cloud.

"This is nice," he commented. "Very nice. A place like this might tempt even me into coming home once in a while."

Once in a while.

The phrase echoed in Sheryl's head as she shoved the key into the lock. If she'd needed anything more to banish the doubts that had plagued her a few moments ago, that would have done it. She had no use for men who returned home every few weeks or months and stayed only long enough to get their laundry done.

"It's comfortable," she replied with deliberate casualness. "And I like the view. From the back patio, you can see— Oh, no!"

She halted in the entryway, aghast. Dirty laundry trailed in a colorful array from the foyer to the living room. Bras, panties, socks, tank tops and uniform shirts decorated the tiles, along with what looked like every shoe she owned.

"Button?" Harry inquired from behind her.

"No," Sheryl said in a huff. Slamming the door, she tossed her purse and her keys on the kitchen counter and bent to scoop up an armful of underwear. "This is the latest decorating scheme for working women who have to dress on the run."

"It works for me."

At his amused comment, she shot a glance over her shoulder. Her face heated when she spied the filmy, chocolate-and-ecru lace bra dangling from his hand. She'd splurged on the bra and matching panties just last week. As any woman who'd ever had to wear a uniform to work could attest, a touch of sinfully decadent silk under the standard, company-issued outer items did wonders for one's inner femininity.

"I'll take that." She snatched the bra out of his hand. "Why don't you wade through this stuff and go into the living room. Since we haven't heard a peep out of Butty-boo, he's obviously—"

"Butty-boo?"

"That's what Inga called him, among other, similarly

nauseating names. He must be hiding." She started down the hall. "You check the living room. I'll check the bedroom."

She found the shih tzu stretched out in regal abandon on her bed. He'd made a nest of the handwoven Zuni blanket she used as a spread. His black-and-white fur blended in with the striking pattern on the blanket, and she might have missed him completely if he hadn't lifted his head at her entrance and given a lazy, half-hearted bark.

"That's it?" Sheryl demanded indignantly. "Two people walk into the house who could be burglars for all you know, and that's the best you can do? One little yip?"

In answer, Button yawned and plopped his head back down.

"Had a hard day, did you?"

Disgusted, she used one foot to right the overturned straw basket she used as a clothes hamper.

"Well, so did I, and I'm telling you here and now that I'd better not come home to any more messes like this one."

With that totally useless warning, Sheryl dumped her laundry in the basket and steeled herself to check the bathroom. To her surprise and considerable relief, Button had used the newspapers she'd spread across the tiles. She hoped that meant he hadn't also used the living-room carpet.

She took a few moments to swipe a little powder on her shiny nose and tuck some stray tendrils of hair back behind her ear, then headed for the living room.

Button's black eyes followed her across the room. With another yawn and an elaborate stretch, he climbed out of his nest, leaped down from the bed and padded after her.

Sheryl had taken only a step or two into the living room when the dog gave a shrill bark that seemed to pierce right through her eardrums. Like a small, furry cannonball, Button launched himself across the mauve carpet at the figure jimmying the locks on the sliding-glass patio doors.

This time, Harry met the attack head-on. Jerking around, he growled at the oncoming canine.

"Take another bite out of my leg and you're history, pal!"

The shih tzu halted a few paces away, every hair bristling.

His target bristled a bit himself. "If it were up to me, you'd be chowing down at the pound right now, so back off. Back off, I said!"

Button didn't take kindly to ultimatums. His black lips drew back even farther. Bug eyes showed red with suppressed fury. The growls that came from deep in his throat grew even more menacing. Guessing that the standoff might break at any second, Sheryl hurried forward and scooped the dog into her arms.

"This is Harry, remember? He's one of the good guys. Well, not a good guy to you, since he sent your mistress off in handcuffs, but he's okay. Really."

Murmuring reassurances, she stroked the small, quivering bundle of fur.

"Helluva watchdog," the marshal muttered in

disgust. "What was he doing back there, anyway? Trying on the rest of your underwear?"

Despite the fact that she herself didn't feel particularly benevolent toward the animal, Sheryl didn't have the heart to expose him to more criticism. Harry didn't need to know that Button had sprawled in indolent indifference while persons unknown had entered her apartment. Besides, the dog had leaped to the attack quickly enough once roused. Deciding to treat the marshal's question as rhetorical, she didn't bother to answer.

"How are the locks?"

"The dead bolt on the front door is sturdy enough. These patio doors are another story. If you don't mind, I'd like to get some security people up here to install a drop bar and kick lock, as well as a rudimentary alarm system. I'll have them wire your car while they're at it. They can be here in an hour or so."

"Tonight?"

"Tonight."

Sheryl's fingers curled into the dog's silky topknot. The fear that had gripped her for a few paralyzing moments in the parking lot reached out long tentacles once more. She shivered.

Harry's keen glance caught the small movement. He gave a smothered oath. "My paranoia's working overtime. The alarm probably isn't necessary, but I'd feel better with it in."

"Probably?" she repeated hollowly.

Harry cursed again and closed the short distance between them. Button issued a warning growl, which the marshal ignored. Lifting a hand, he smoothed an errant curl back from her cheek.

"I'm sorry, Sher. I didn't mean to scare you again."

The touch of his palm against her cheek startled Sheryl so much that she barely noticed his use of her nickname. She did, however, notice the tiny bits of gold warming his brown eyes. And the way his mustache thickened slightly at the corners, as if to disguise the small, curving laugh lines that appeared whenever his mouth kicked into one of his half-rogue, all-male grins.

The way it did now.

Except this grin was more rueful than roguish. It matched the look in his eyes, Sheryl thought, as his hand slid slowly from her cheek to curl back of her neck.

She shivered once more, but this time it wasn't from fear. This time, she realized with something close to dismay, it was from delight. Caught on a confusing cross of sensations, she could only stand and watch the way Harry's grin tipped from rueful into a smile that trapped her breath in the back of her throat.

He shouldn't do this! Harry's mind shouted the warning, even as his fingers got lost in the silky softness of her hair. He knew better than to mix business with personal desire. But suddenly, without the least warning, desire had grabbed hold of him and wouldn't let go.

She felt so soft. Smelled so intoxicating, a mixture of hot sun and powdery talcum, with a little shih tzu thrown in for leavening. She was also scared, Harry reminded himself savagely. Off balance from all that had happened in the past few days. Almost engaged.

Another man might have drawn back at that sobering thought. Someone else might have respected the territory this Brian character had tentatively staked out. Instead of deterring Harry, the very nebulousness of the other man's claim angered him. Any jerk who kept a woman like Sheryl dangling in some twilight never-never land didn't deserve her.

So when she didn't draw back, when her lips opened on a sigh instead of a protest, Harry bent his head and brushed them with his own. She tasted so fresh, so irresistible, that he brought his mouth back for another sample.

The kiss started out slow and soft and friendly. Within seconds, it powered up to fast and hard and well beyond friendship. A dozen different sensations exploded in Harry's chest and belly. The urge to pull Sheryl into his arms, to feel every inch of her against his length, clawed at him. He started to do just that when another, sharper sensation bit into his lower right arm.

"Dammit!"

He jumped back, almost yanking the stubby little monster locked onto his jacket sleeve out of Sheryl's arms. She caught the dog just in time and held on to it by its rear legs. It hung there between them, a growling, snarling mop with one end firmly attached to Harry's sleeve and the other to the woman who held him.

"You misbegotten, mangy little…"

"He was just trying to protect me," Sheryl got out on a gasp. "I think."

Harry thought differently, but he was too busy

working his fingers onto either side of the dog's muzzle to say so at that moment. Exerting just enough pressure to spring those tiny, steel jaws open, he pulled his coat sleeve free. He then reached over and extracted the animal from Sheryl's unresisting arms.

Two long strides took him back to the sliding doors. A moment later, the glass panel slammed shut. Buggy black eyes glared at him from the outside. Ignoring the glare and the bad-tempered yips that accompanied it, Harry turned back to Sheryl.

His fierce, driving need to sweep her into his arms once more took a direct hit when he caught her expression. It held a combination of regret and guilt…and not the least hint of any invitation to continue.

Chapter 6

"I'm sorry."

The apology came out with a gruffer edge than Harry had intended, for the simple reason that he couldn't think of anything he felt less sorry about than taking Sheryl into his arms. Yet that kiss ranked right up there among the dumbest things he'd ever done.

That said something, considering that he'd pulled some real boners in his life. Two in particular he'd always regret. The first was succumbing to a bad case of lust and marrying too young, much too young to figure out how to get his struggling marriage through the stress of his job. The second occurred years later, when he decided to take a few long-overdue days off to go fishing in Canada. That fateful weekend his best buddy was gunned down. By the time Harry had returned and taken charge of the operation to track down Dean's killers, the trail had gone stone cold.

Now it had finally heated up, and he couldn't allow himself to get sidetracked by a moss-eyed blonde who raised his blood pressure a half-dozen points every time she glanced his way. Nor, he reminded himself with deliberate ruthlessness, could he afford to confuse her by coming on to her like this. He needed her calm and rational and able to concentrate on the task she'd been detailed to do. She still had information Harry wanted to pull out of her.

"That was out of line," he admitted, less gruffly, more firmly. "It won't happen again."

"N-no. It won't."

The guilt in her voice rubbed him raw. Cursing the predatory instincts that had driven him to poach so recklessly on another man's territory, he tried to recapture her trust.

"I guess this damned investigation has sanded away the few civilized edges I possessed."

It had sanded away a few of Sheryl's edges, too. She couldn't remember the last time a kiss had seared her like that. Dazed, she struggled to subdue the runaway fire racing through her veins. A massive dose of guilt helped speed the process considerably.

She was almost engaged, for heaven's sake! How could she have just stood there and let Harry kiss her like that? How could she have been so shallow, so disloyal to Brian? She'd never even looked at another man in all the time they'd been seeing each other. What's more, she'd certainly never dreamed that a near stranger could generate this combination of singing excitement and stinging regret with just the touch of his mouth on hers. She stared at Harry, seeing her own consternation in his frown.

"We've got a good number of hours of work ahead of us yet," he got out curtly. "You can't concentrate if you're worried that I might pounce at any minute. I won't, I promise."

A small sense of pique piled on top of Sheryl's rapidly mounting guilt. She knew darn well she was as much to blame for what had just happened as Harry. Her instinctive, uninhibited response to his touch shook her to her core, and she didn't need him to tell her it wouldn't happen again. She wouldn't do that to Brian or to herself. Still, it rankled just a bit that the marshal regretted their kiss as much as she did, if for entirely different reasons.

Feeling flustered and thoroughly off balance, Sheryl had a need to put some distance between her and Harry. She moved into the kitchen, where she snatched up Button's plastic water dish and shoved it under the faucet to rinse it out.

"Why don't you head back downtown," she suggested with what she hoped was a credible semblance of calm. "I'll follow after I feed Button, and we can put in a few more hours' work."

Harry looked as though there was nothing he'd like better than to get back to business, but he shook his head. "I'd like to stay here until the security folks arrive and do their thing, if you don't mind."

Sheryl stared at him while water ran over the sides

of the dish. In the aftermath of his shattering kiss, she'd totally forgotten what had led up to it.

"No, of course I don't mind."

"I'll call them and get them on the way."

With brisk efficiency, he mobilized the necessary specialists. Another quick call alerted Ev to the fact that he'd have to scrounge his own dinner.

"I guess I could make us some sandwiches," Sheryl said slowly when he snapped the phone shut. "Or I could cook lemon chicken. I have all the fixings. We can eat and work while we wait."

The idea of preparing Brian's favorite meal for Harry disconcerted Sheryl all over again. Honestly, she had to get a grip here. Harry had certainly recovered his poise fast enough. He'd faced the awkwardness head-on and moved beyond it. She could do the same. Briskly, she swiped a paper towel around the bowl and filled it with the dried dog food she'd picked up yesterday.

"I'll feed Button and get something started."

"I have a better idea." Harry shrugged out of his coat, then rolled up his sleeves. "You feed the rodent while I pour you a glass of wine or whatever relaxes you. Then I'll cook the chicken."

"There's some wine in the fridge," Sheryl said doubtfully, "but you don't have to fix dinner."

"I don't have to, but I'd like to."

He flashed her a grin that strung her tummy into tight knots. Good grief, what in the world was the matter with her?

"Being on the road so much, I don't get to practice my culinary skills very often. But my ex-wife trained me well. She never opened a can or flipped on a burner when I was home."

"Well…"

He traded places with Sheryl, taking over the kitchen with an easy competence that put the last of her doubts to rest. A quick investigation of her cupboards and fridge produced skillet, chicken, flour, lemons, onions, cracked pepper, butter and a half-full bottle of chilled Chablis.

While Harry assembled the necessary ingredients, Sheryl fed Button. Naturally, the dog displayed his displeasure over his banishment to the patio by turning up his pug nose at the dry food. She left him and his dinner outside, then occupied one of the tall rawhide-and-rattan counter stools. Sipping slowly on the wine Harry had poured for her, she tried to understand the welter of confused emotions this man stirred in her.

She gave up after the second or third sip and contented herself with just watching. He hadn't been kidding about his culinary skills. Within moments, he had the floured chicken fillets sizzling in the skillet. While they browned, he made short work of dicing the onion. Seconds later, the onion, more butter and a generous dollop of Chablis went into the pan. Sheryl sniffed the delicious combination of scents, conscious once more of the inadequacy of the Korn Kurls she'd eaten for lunch.

"My compliments to your ex-wife," she murmured. "You really do know your way around a kitchen."

"Unfortunately, cooking is my one and only domestic skill…or so I've been told."

"How long were you married?" she asked curiously.

He squeezed a wedge of lemon over the chicken. The drops spurted and spit in the hot pan, adding their tangy scent to the aroma of butter and onions rising from the cooktop.

"Eight years by calendar reckoning. Three, maybe four, if you count the time my wife and I spent at home together. She's an account executive for a Dallas PR firm now, but when we met she was just starting in the business. Her job took her on the road as much as mine did, and…"

"And constant absences don't necessarily make the heart grow fonder," she finished slowly.

He shrugged, but Sheryl had been in this man's company enough by now to catch the tight note in his voice. Harry MacMillan didn't give up on anything easily, she now knew, whether it was a marriage or the relentless pursuit of a fugitive.

"Something like that," he concurred, sending her a keen glance through the spiraling steam. "You sound as though you've been there, too."

"In a way."

She traced a circle on the counter with her glass. She rarely spoke about the father whose absence had left such a void in her heart, but Harry's blunt honesty about his divorce invited reciprocation. Reluctantly, she shared a little of her own background.

"My father traveled a lot in his job, too. My mother stewed and fretted every minute he was gone, which didn't make for happy homecomings."

"I imagine not. Is he still on the road?"

"As far as I know. He and Mom divorced when I was

six. He showed up for a Christmas or two, and we wrote each other until I was about ten. The letters got fewer and farther between after he took an overseas position. Last I heard, he was in Oman."

"Want me to track him down for you? It would only take a few calls."

He was serious, Sheryl saw with a little gulp.

"No, thanks," she said hastily. "I don't need him wandering in and out of my life anymore."

"Well, the offer stands if you change your mind," he replied, flipping the slotted wooden spoon into the air like a baton. He caught it with a smooth ripple of white shirt and lean muscle. "Do you have any rice in the cupboard? I'm even better at rice Marconi than lemon chicken."

"And so modest, too."

He grinned. "Modesty isn't one of the skills they emphasize in the academy. Relax, enjoy your wine and watch a master at work."

Maybe it was the Chablis. Or the sight of this tall, rangy man moving so matter-of-factly about her little kitchen. In any case, Sheryl relaxed, enjoyed her wine and managed to ignore the fact that the master chef sported a leather shoulder holster instead of a tall, white hat. Her prickly sense of guilt stayed with her, though, and kept her from completely enjoying the meal Harry served up with a flourish.

It also kept her on the other side of the dining-room table after they finished eating and got down to work. Button, released from his banishment, perched on the back of the sofa and watched the marshal with unblinking, unwavering hostility. With the wine and food to soothe the nerves made ragged by Harry's kiss, Sheryl was able to recall the details on several batches of postcards.

"Venice, the Antibes, Barbados." Harry tapped his pen on the tabletop. "You're sure the cards that arrived before the Rio set came from those three locations?"

"I'm sure. It's hard to mistake gondolas and canals. I remember Antibes because of the little gold emblem in the corner of the card that advertised the Côte d'Azur. And Barbados..."

Sheryl gazed at the wall, seeing in its wavy plaster a sea so polished it glittered like clear, blue topaz, and white beaches lined with banyan trees whose roots hung downward like long, scraggly beards.

"If the picture on the card came anywhere close to reality," she murmured, "Barbados must have the most beautiful beaches in the world."

Harry's pen stilled. Against his will, against his better judgment, he let his glance linger on Sheryl's face. Damn, didn't the woman have any idea what that soft, dreamy expression did to a man's concentration? Or how much of herself she revealed in these unguarded moments? Despite her assertions to the contrary, Harry suspected that the daughter had inherited more than a touch of her father's wanderlust. She tried hard to suppress it, but it slipped out in moments like this, when she mentally transported herself to a white sweep of beach.

Despite *his* intentions to the contrary, Harry mentally transported himself there with her.

The sound of a low, rumbling growl wrenched him back to Albuquerque. A quick look revealed that Button had shifted his attention from Harry to the front door. The dog's entire body quivered as he pushed up on all four paws and stared at the entryway. His gums pulled back. Another low growl rattled in his throat.

Carefully, Harry laid down his pen. "Are you expecting anyone?"

Sheryl's eyes widened at his soft query. Gulping, she shifted her gaze to the door. "No," she whispered.

"Stay here!"

Harry moved toward the door, his mind spinning with possibilities. The dog might have alerted on a neighbor arriving home. Maybe the security team was outside. Whoever it was, Harry had been a cop too long to take a chance on mights and maybes. He waited in the entryway, his every sense straining.

He heard no murmur of voices, no passing footsteps, no doorbell. Only Button's quivering growls…and a small, almost inaudible scrape.

Pulse pounding, back to the wall, Harry edged toward the door. With no side windows to peer out, he had to resort to the peephole. He made out a bent head, a pale blur of a shirt, a glint of moonlight on steel.

With a kick to his gut, he saw the dead bolt slowly twist.

His hand whipped across his chest. The Smith & Wesson came out of its leather nest with a smooth, familiar slide. He reached for the doorknob and waited until the dead bolt clicked open.

The knob moved under his palm. He exploded into action at the exact instant Button flew off the sofa, snarling, and Sheryl shouted at him.

"Harry! Wait!"

Her cry was still echoing in his ears when he yanked the door open with his free hand. A second later, the stranger standing on the other side of the door slammed up against the hallway wall. The Smith & Wesson dug into his ribs.

His cheek squashed into the plaster, the tall, slender man couldn't do much more than gape over his shoulder at his attacker.

"Wh— What's going on here?" he stuttered. "Who are you?"

In response, Harry torqued the stranger's arm up his spine another few inches. His adrenaline pumped like high-octane jet fuel. Button's high-pitched yaps scratched on his strung-tight nerves like fingernails on a chalkboard.

"You first," he countered roughly. "Who the hell are you?"

Before he got an answer, Sheryl locked both hands on his arm. "It's Brian," she shouted, yanking at his bruising hold. "Let go, Harry. It's Brian. Brian Mitchell."

Slowly, he released his grip and stepped back. Button didn't give up as readily. It took Sheryl's direct intervention before the still-snarling dog retired from the field. A good-sized strip of gray twill pants dangled from his locked jaws.

The two men faced each other, blood still up and faces flushed. Sheryl dumped the dog on the sofa and hurried back to calm the roiled waters.

"Brian, I'm so sorry! I didn't expect you, and it's been such a crazy day. Are you okay? Button didn't break the skin on your leg, did he?"

"No." Jaw clamped, the younger man watched his attacker holster his gun. "Who's this?"

"This is, er…" She turned, her face a study in frustration. "I can tell him, can't I?"

Harry took his time replying. Now that he knew the man didn't pose an immediate threat, his sharp-edged tension should have eased. Instead, Sheryl's fluttering and fussing raised his hackles all over again. It didn't take any great deductive skills to identify the man as Brian, her almost-fiancé.

Eyes glinting, he assessed the newcomer. An inch or two shorter than Harry's own six-one, he carried a good deal less weight on his trim frame. He also, the marshal noted, didn't take kindly to having his face shoved up against the wall.

"Elise said someone came into the station this morning and pulled you for a special detail. I take it this is the guy."

"Yes."

His gaze sliced from Sheryl to Harry. "Working kind of late, aren't you?"

She answered for them, a tinge of pink in her cheeks. "Yes, we are. Why don't you come in? I want to check your leg to make sure Button didn't do any serious damage."

Unmoving, Brian looked the marshal up and down. His lip curled. "I wouldn't have picked you for a shih tzu owner."

"You got that much right, anyway," Harry replied with a careless shrug. "I would have dumped the mutt in the pound. Sher insisted on bringing it home."

He used the nickname deliberately, not exactly sure why he wanted to get a rise out of the younger man. Whatever the reason, Brian's scowl sent a spear of satisfaction through his belly.

Sheryl listened to their terse exchange with increasing consternation flavored with a pinch of irritation. They sounded like two boys baiting each other. She could understand why Brian might feel antagonistic, given Harry's rough handling and his presence in her apartment so late at night, but she could do without the marshal's deliberate provocation.

"Let's go into the living room," she said firmly. "Harry will explain what we're doing while I check your leg."

The remains of the meal still sitting on the table didn't help matters, of course. Nor did the empty wine bottle on the kitchen counter. Frowning, Brian took in the littered table, the half-empty wineglasses and the dog once more stretched along the back of the sofa, his duty done. Slowly, he turned to face Sheryl.

"My leg's fine," he said quietly, all trace of antagonism gone now. "But I can certainly use a little explaining."

Before she could reply, Harry stepped forward. The gold star gleamed from the leather credentials case lying in his palm.

"I'm Deputy U.S. Marshal Harry MacMillan. Since Sheryl vouches for you, I'll tell you that I'm tracking a fugitive who escaped while being transported for trial a year ago. His trail led to Albuquerque and, obliquely, to the Monzano branch of the post office."

Brian's face registered blank astonishment, followed by swift concern. "Is this fugitive dangerous?"

"He's suspected of killing the marshal escorting him to trial."

"And you pulled Sheryl into a hunt for a cop killer?"

"I requested that she be assigned to my team, yes."

"Well, you can just unrequest her," Brian declared. "I don't want her taking part in any manhunt for a cop killer."

Sheryl gave a little huff of exasperation. "Ex-cuse me. I'm getting a little tired of this two-sided conversation. In case you've forgotten, this is my apartment and my living room, and it's my decision whether or not I'm going to work on this detail."

Brian conceded her point stiffly. "Of course it's your decision, but I don't like it. Aside from the possible danger, this detail of yours has already disrupted our schedule. I waited almost an hour for you yesterday afternoon, and we missed our Tuesday night together."

As she looked up into his gray eyes, Sheryl's momentary irritation disappeared, swept away by a fresh wave of guilt. She loved Brian. She'd loved him for almost a year now. Yet she'd gotten so caught up in Harry's investigation that she hadn't spared much thought to this kind, considerate man—until the marshal kissed her.

She felt a sudden, urgent need to fold herself into Brian's arms and feel his mouth on hers. She turned, offering Harry a forced smile. "Would you keep Button entertained for a few minutes? I'm going to walk Brian to his car."

"You stay here and talk," he countered. "Much as I hate to be seen in public with this sorry excuse for a dog, he can keep me company while I reconnoiter the outside layout for the security folks."

Sheryl grabbed the leash she'd purchased when she bought the dog food and shoved it in his hand gratefully. Frowning, Brian watched the oversized marshal depart with the undersized mop of fur at the end of a bright-red lead.

"Security folks?" he echoed as the door closed. "What security folks?"

Sighing, Sheryl abandoned her need to be held in favor of Brian's need to know. Taking a seat beside him on the sofa, she tucked a foot under her and recapped the events of the past few days. When she got to the part about the slashed tires, Brian voiced his growing consternation.

"At the risk of repeating myself, I have to say I don't like this. I wish you'd take yourself off this detail."

"We don't know that my slashed tires had anything to do with my participation on the task force. Anyone could have done it, but Harry insists it's better not to take chances. He's got a team coming out to install new locks and an alarm system."

"I still don't like it," Brian repeated stubbornly.

Sheryl bit back the retort that she'd didn't particularly like that part, either. She probably should feel flattered by Brian's protective streak. Instead, she resented it just a little bit. No, more than a little bit.

Suddenly, Sheryl remembered that she'd curled into Harry's side for protection only this afternoon, without feeling the least hint of resentment.

Guilt, confusion and a desperate need to reestablish her usual sense of comfortable ease with Brian brought her forward. Sliding her arms around his neck, she smiled up at him.

"I'm sorry you don't like it, and I appreciate your concern. I want to be part of this team, though. If I have any knowledge that could lead to the capture of a murderer, I have to share it. After this detail, we'll get back to our regular routine. I promise."

Conceding with his usual good-natured grace, he bent his head and met her halfway. Their mouths fit together with practiced sureness…and none of the explosive excitement that Sheryl had experienced only a half hour ago.

Dismayed, she rose up on her knees. Her body melted against Brian's. Her fingers tunneled through his hair. Brian was more than willing to deepen the embrace. His arms went around her waist, drawing her closer.

Afterward, she could never sort out whether he pulled back first or she did. Nor would she ever forget the look in his eyes. Puzzled. Surprised. Not hurt, but close. Too close.

"I guess I'd better leave," he said slowly. "So you and—what's his name?—Harry can get back to work."

When his arms dropped away, her ache spread into a slow, lancing pain. Deep within her, she knew that she would never find her usual comfortable satisfaction in his embrace again. She'd changed. Somehow, she'd become a different person.

She loved Brian. She would always love him. But she knew now that she'd mistaken the nature of that love. Comfort didn't form the basis for a marriage. Security couldn't ensure happiness. For either of them.

If nothing else, Harry's searing kiss had demonstrated that. Sheryl didn't fool herself that she'd fallen in love with Harry MacMillan, or even in lust. She'd barely known the man for thirty-six hours. Yet in that brief period, he'd knocked the foundations right out from under Sheryl's nice, placid existence.

Aching, she wet her lips and tried to articulate some of her confused thoughts.

"Brian…"

He shook his head. "I need to do some thinking. I guess you do, too. We'll talk about it when you finish this detail, Sher."

He pushed himself off the sofa. Miserable, Sheryl followed him to the door. He paused, one hand on the knob, as reluctant to walk out as she was to let him.

"Elise said you rescheduled your shopping expedition for a bassinet for tomorrow night. You need to call her if you're going to be working late again."

"I will." She grabbed at the excuse to delay his departure for another few moments. "Or maybe you could take her?"

He nodded. "Sure, if you can't make it. And don't forget to call your mother. You know she expects to hear from you every Thursday."

"I won't."

He opened the door, and a small silence fell between them. Sheryl felt her heart splinter into tiny shards of pain when he curled a hand under her chin.

"Bye, Sher," he said softly.

"Goodbye, Brian."

He tilted her head up for a final kiss.

* * *

Harry watched from the shadows across the court-yard. He needed to see this, he thought, his jaw tight. He needed the physical evidence of Brian's claim. Of Sheryl's affection.

It made Harry's own relationship with her easier, clearer, sharper. She was part of his team.

Nothing more.

Nothing less.

Which didn't explain why he had to battle the irrational temptation to unclip Button's leash and turn the man-eating fur ball loose on Brian Mitchell again.

Chapter 7

Sheryl walked into the task force operations center twenty minutes late on Thursday morning. A taut, unsmiling Harry greeted her.

"Where the hell have you been? I was about to send a squad car up to your place to check on you."

"Button set the darn alarm off twice before I figured out how to bypass the motion detectors."

The marshal bit back what Sheryl suspected was another biting comment about hairy little rodents. Instead, he raked her with a glance that left small scorch marks everywhere it touched her skin.

"Call in the next time you have a problem."

The curt order raised her brows and her hackles. "Yes, sir!"

Harry narrowed his eyes but didn't respond.

Tossing her purse onto a chair, Sheryl headed for the coffeepot in the corner of the conference room. She didn't know what had gotten into Harry this morning, but his uncertain mood more than matched her own. She felt grouchy and irritable and unaccountably off-kilter in the marshal's presence.

Much of her edginess she could ascribe to the fact that she hadn't gotten much sleep last night. She'd spent countless hours tossing and turning and thinking about Brian. She'd spent almost as many hours trying *not* to think about Harry's shattering kiss. She couldn't, wouldn't, allow herself to dwell on the sensations the marshal had roused in her, not when she owed Brian her loyalty.

To make matters even worse, Button had added his bit to her restless night. The mutt insisted on burrowing under the covers and curling up in the bend of her knees. Every time Sheryl had tried to straighten her legs, she'd disturbed his slumber…a move that Button didn't particularly appreciate. He'd voiced his displeasure in no uncertain terms. Between the dog's growls and her own troubled thoughts, Sheryl was sure she'd barely closed her eyes for an hour or so before the alarm went off.

Grumbling, she'd dragged out of bed, pulled on a pair of white slacks and a cool, sleeveless silk blouse in a bright ruby red, then grabbed a glass of juice and a slice of toast. She still might have made it down to the federal building by eight if she'd hadn't had to struggle with the unfamiliar alarm system. Twenty minutes and three calls to the alarm company later, she'd slammed the door behind her and headed for her car.

Her day hadn't gotten off to a good start, even before Harry's curt greeting. As she greeted the assembled team members, she guessed that it wouldn't get much better.

Crisp and professional in her New Mexico state trooper's uniform, Fay Chandler shook her head in response to Sheryl's query about her son's T-ball game.

"They got creamed," she said glumly. "I had to take the whole team for pizza to cheer them up. They perked up at the first whiff of pepperoni, but my husband was still moping when I left the house this morning. He's worse than my seven-year-old."

Folding her hands around the hot, steaming coffee, Sheryl took cautious injections of the liquid caffeine. She carried the cup with her to the conference table and greeted Everett Sloan. The poor man was almost buried behind a stack of computer printouts.

"Hi, Ev. Looks like you're hard at it already."

The short, barrel-chested deputy marshal waved a half-eaten chocolate donut. "'Hard' is the operative word. The computers crunched the numbers and words you gave us from the first set of postcards. Take a look at what they kicked out."

Sheryl's eyes widened at the row of cardboard boxes stacked along one wall, each filled with neatly folded printouts.

"Good grief! Do you have to go through all those?"

"Every one of them."

"What in the world are they?"

"We bounced the numbers and letters of the words you gave us against the known codes maintained by the

FBI and Defense Intelligence Agency to see if there's a pattern. So far, no luck." Grimacing, he surveyed the boxes still awaiting his attention. "It'll take until Christmas to find a needle in that haystack…if there is one."

"We don't have until Christmas," Harry put in from the other end of the table. "We've got to break that code fast. We caught Inga Gunderson with her bags packed, remember? We have to assume the drop is scheduled for sometime soon…if it hasn't already gone down," he added grimly.

Fay hitched a hip on the edge of the conference table. "My bet is that Inga sent a message through her lawyer. She probably alerted either the sender or the receivers to the fact she's been tagged. If they didn't call off the shipment, they've no doubt diverted it to an alternate location."

Ev shook his head. "I know her lawyer. Several of us in the Albuquerque Marshals' office had to provide extra courtroom security when he defended one of his skinhead clients against a charge of communicating a threat against a federal law enforcement official. The scuzzball swore his buddies would blow up the Federal building if he was found guilty."

Since the Oklahoma City bombing, Sheryl knew, those threats were taken very, very seriously. She remembered the tension that had gripped the city during that trial.

"Don Ortega gave the guy one helluva defense," Ev continued, "but he told me afterward he fully expected to go up in smoke with his client. He's tough but straight. He wouldn't knowingly aid an escaped prisoner or contribute to the commission of a crime."

"But he might do it unknowingly," Fay argued. "Maybe Inga and company used some kind of a coded message. They're certainly handy enough at that sort of thing."

Ev shook his head emphatically. "Not Don. He's too smart to act as a courier for a suspected felon. Besides, the supervisor of the women's detention center swears Inga hasn't made any calls to anyone other than her attorney. So the odds are that the drop is still on…for a time we've yet to determine at a place we haven't identified."

"We'll identify both," Harry swore, his face as tight and determined as his voice. "Keep working those computer reports. If you don't find anything that makes sense, run them again with the day-month combinations for the next five days."

His partner groaned. "I'm going to need more energy for this."

Polishing off his donut, Ev dug another out of the box in the center of the table. While he munched his way through the report in front of him, Harry turned to the state trooper.

"I want you to drive out to all the airports we've IDed as possible landing sites. Talk to the Customs people and airport managers personally. Ask them to info us on any flight plans with South America as originating departure point or cargo manifests showing transport from or through Rio. Also, tell them to notify us immediately of any unscheduled requests for transit servicing on aircraft large enough to carry this kind of a cargo load."

Fay reached for her Smoky the Bear hat. "Will do, Chief."

Topping off his coffee, Harry walked back to his seat. "All right, Sheryl, let's get to work."

She shot him a quick glance as she settled in the chair next to his. He'd shed his jacket, but otherwise wore his standard uniform of boots, jeans and button-down cotton shirt, this one a soft, faded yellow. His clean-shaven jaw and neatly trimmed mustache looked crisply professional, but the lines at the corners of his eyes and mouth suggested that he'd hadn't slept much more than she had.

No doubt his investigation had kept him awake. It certainly seemed to consume him this morning. He gave no sign that he even remembered brushing a hand across her cheek last night or sending her into a shivering, shuddering nosedive with the touch of his mouth on hers. Not that Sheryl wanted him to remember, of course, any more than she wanted him to kiss her again.

Not until she'd sorted out her feelings for Brian, anyway.

"Where do you want to start?" she asked briskly.

"Let's go over the wording from the Venice-Antibes-Barbados cards again. Start with Barbados."

"Fine."

They worked for several hours before Harry was sat-isfied that he'd extracted all the information he could on that set of postcards. After sending the key words down to the computer center for analysis, they moved on to other cards that had arrived during Inga Gunder-son's four months in Albuquerque. The further back Sheryl reached into her memory, the hazier the dates and stamps and messages got. The scenes on the front side of the cards remained vivid, however.

"Give me what you can on this one from Heidelberg," Harry instructed.

"It came in early April, a week or so before the fifteenth. I remember that much, because it provided such a colorful counterpoint to all the dreary income tax returns we had to sort and process."

Harry scribbled a note. "Go on."

"It was one of my favorites. It had four different scenes on the front. One showed a fairy tale castle perched above the Neckar River. Another depicted the old bridge that spans the river. Then there was a group of university students lifting their beer steins and singing, just like Mario Lanza and his friends did in the *Student Prince*."

At the other end of the table, Ev groaned. "Mario Lanza and the *Student Prince*. I can just imagine what the computers will do with that one!"

Harry ignored him. "What about the fourth scene?"

"That was the best." Sheryl assembled her thoughts. "It showed a monstrous wine cask in the basement of the castle. According to Paul's note, the cask holds something like fifty thousand gallons. Supposedly, the king's dwarf once drained the whole thing."

Harry stared at her. A slow, almost reluctant approval dawned in his eyes, warming them to honey brown. "Fifty thousand gallons, huh? That gives us an interesting number to work with. Good going, Sher."

For the first time that morning, Sheryl relaxed. A sense of partnership, of shared purpose, replaced her earlier irritation with Harry's brusque manner. When he wasn't glowering at her or barking out orders, the marshal had his own brand of rough-edged charm.

As she'd discovered last night.

From the other end of the table, Ev whistled softly. "How the heck can you remember that kind of detail?"

"A good memory is one of the primary qualifications for a postal worker," she replied, smiling. "Especially those of us who are scheme qualified."

"Okay, I'll bite. What's 'scheme qualified'?"

"Although I primarily work the front counter, I'm also authorized to come in early and help throw mail for the carrier runs. Everything arrives in bulk from the central distribution center, you see, then we have to sort it by zip."

"I thought you had machines to do that."

"I wish!" Sheryl laughed. "No, most of the mail is hand-thrown at the branch level. I worked at two different Albuquerque stations before I moved to the Monzano branch. I can pretty well tell you the zip for any street you pick out of the phone book," she finished smugly.

"No kidding?"

Ev looked as though he wanted to put her to the test, but Harry intervened.

"Unless they're pertinent to this investigation, I'm not interested in any zips but the ones on these postcards. Let's get back to work."

"Yes, sir!" Ev and Sheryl chorused.

Harry grilled her relentlessly, extracting every detail she could remember about Mrs. Gunderson's correspondence and then some. They worked steadily, despite constant interruptions.

The phones in the task force operations center rang frequently. In one call, the DEA advised that the informant who'd tipped them to Paul and Inga Gunderson had just come up with another name. They were working to ID the man now. Just before noon, the CIA came back with an unconfirmed field report that six canisters of depleted uranium had indeed passed through Prague four days ago. Their contact was still working Pamplona and Rio to see if he could pick up the trail. His face alive with fierce satisfaction, Harry reported the news to his small team.

"Hot damn!" Ev exclaimed. "Prague! Good going, Sheryl."

A thrill shot through her. She couldn't believe the information she'd provided only yesterday had already borne fruit. Her eyes met Harry's above his latest ream of notes.

"I owe you," he said quietly. "Big time."

Her skin tingled everywhere his gaze touched it. She smiled, and answered just as softly.

"All in the line of duty, Marshal."

The call that came in from their contact in the APD a little later took some of the edge off Sheryl's sense of satisfaction. The police hadn't turned up any leads regarding her slashed tires, nor had they located the man who'd hassled her yesterday morning over his girlfriend's welfare check. The woman had moved, and none of the neighbors knew her or her boyfriend's current address.

"They're going to keep working it," Harry advised.

"I hope so."

In addition to the many incoming calls, the task force also had a number of visitors, including the deputy U.S. district attorney working the charges against Inga Gunderson. Harry and Ev conferred with the man in private for some time. Just before noon, the three of them went downstairs for Inga Gunderson's custody hearing. The marshals returned an hour later, elated and more determined than ever. The government's lawyer had convinced the judge to hold Inga pending a grand-jury review of the charges against her, they reported. The good guys had won another two, possibly three days while the woman remained in custody.

"That's great for you," Sheryl said with a sigh, "but it looks like I've got Button for at least two, possibly three, more days."

"There's always the pound," Harry reminded her.

When she declined to reply, Ev picked up on the conversation.

"Inga's attorney asked about the dog. Said his client was worried about her precious Butty-Boo. We assured him the mutt was in good hands." His pudgy face took on a thoughtful air. "Maybe we should check the mutt out again."

Harry's head jerked up sharply. "You said you went over him while we were at Inga's house."

"I took his collar apart and searched what I could of his fur without losing all ten of my fingers. I might have missed something."

"Great."

"Or he could be carrying something internally," Ev finished with a grimace. He eyed the other marshal across the table. "I'll let you handle this one, MacMillan. You lugged the mutt around under your arm for most of yesterday. He knows you."

"I've done a lot of things in the pursuit of justice," Harry drawled, "but I draw the line at a body cavity search of a fuzz ball with teeth. If you don't mind giving me your house keys and the alarm code, Sheryl, I'll send a squad car out to pick him up and take him to the vet who works the drug dogs. He's got full X-ray capability."

Sheryl dug her keys out of her purse, then passed them across the table. Poor Button. She suspected he wouldn't enjoy the next hour or so. Neither would the vet.

Harry dispatched the squad car, resumed his seat next to hers and reviewed his notes. "Okay, we've got details on eight postcards now. Can you remember any more?"

Sheryl sorted through her memory. "I think there were two, perhaps three, more."

They worked steadily for another hour. A uniformed police officer returned Sheryl's keys and a report that the dog was clean. Fay Chandler called in from Farmington, where she was waiting for the manager of the local airport to make an appearance. Ev went downstairs to confer with his buddies in the computer center.

Finally, Harry leaned back in his chair and tapped his stub of a pencil on his notes. "Well, I guess that's it. We've covered the same ground three times now, with nothing new to add to our list of key words or numbers."

"I wish I could remember more."

"You've given us and the computer wizards downstairs enough to keep us busy the rest of the night. If we don't break whatever code these cards carried, it won't be from lack of trying."

Feeling oddly deflated now that she'd finished her task, Sheryl swept the empty conference room with a glance. After only two days, the litter of phones and maps and computerized printouts seemed as familiar to her as her own living room.

"Do you need me for anything else?"

Harry's gaze drifted over her face for a moment. "If...when...we make sense of what you've told us, I'll give you a call. We might need you to verify some detail. In the meantime, I want you to stay alert...and let me know if any more postcards show up, of course."

"Of course."

"Preferably *before* you return them to sender."

"We'll try to be less efficient," she said gravely.

A small silence gripped them, as though neither wanted to make the next move. Then Harry pushed back his chair.

"I know I've put you through the wringer for the past couple of days. I appreciate the information you've provided, Sheryl. I'll make sure the postmaster knows how much."

He held out his hand. Hers slipped into it with a warm shock that disturbed her almost as much as the realization that she might not see him again after today.

"You'll let me know when...if...Inga gets out of custody, so I can send Button back to her?"

"I will, although if I have my way, that won't occur for seven to ten years, minimum."

"Well…" She tugged her hand free of his.

"I'll walk you down to your car."

Their footsteps echoed in the tiled corridor. Side by side, they waited for the elevator.

Why couldn't he just let her go? Harry wondered. Just let her walk away? There wasn't any need to prolong the contact. He'd gotten what he wanted out of her.

No, his mind mocked, not quite all he wanted.

With every breath he drew in he caught her scent and knew he wanted more from this woman. A lot more. He'd spent most of last night thinking about the feel of her mouth under his, tasting again her wine-flavored kiss. And most of today trying not to notice how her tawny hair curled at her temples, or the way her red silk blouse showed off her golden skin.

If Harry hadn't witnessed the scene in her doorway last night, he might have come back to Albuquerque after he cornered his quarry and given this Brian character a run for his money. But the aching tenderness in Sheryl's face when she'd bid her almost-fiancé goodnight had killed that half-formed idea before it really took root. His predatory instincts might allow him to challenge another male for a woman's interest, but he wouldn't loose those instincts on one so obviously in love with another man…as much as he burned to.

The elevator swooshed open, then carried them downward in a smooth, silent descent. With a smile and a nod to the guard manning the security post, Harry escorted Sheryl to the underground parking garage.

Her little Camry sat waiting in the numbered slot Harry had arranged for her. She deactivated the newly installed alarm with the remote device, unlocked the door and tossed her purse inside. Then she unclipped her temporary badge and handed it to him.

"I guess I won't need this anymore."

His hand fisted over the plastic badge. "Thanks again, Sheryl. You've given me more to work with than I've had in almost a year."

"You're welcome."

Let her go! Dammit, he had to let her go! Deliberately, he stepped back.

"I'll keep you posted on what happens," he said again, more briskly this time. "And what to do with Button."

She took the hint and slid into the car. "Thanks."

Harry closed the door for her and stood in a faint haze of exhaust while Sheryl backed out of the slot and drove up the exit ramp. Turning on one heel, he returned to the conference room.

He made a quick call to the task force's contact in the APD to confirm that they'd keep an eye on the Monzano Street station and Miss Hancock's apartment for the next few days. Then he got back to the glamorous, adventurous work of a U.S. marshal.

"All right, Ev, let me have some of those computer printouts."

They worked until well after midnight. Wire tight from the combination of long hours and a mounting frustration over his inability to break the damned code of the postcards, Harry drove to his motel just off of I-40.

The door slammed shut behind him. The chain latch rattled into place. The puny little chain and flimsy door lock wouldn't keep out a determined ten-year-old, but the .357 Magnum Harry slid out of its holster and laid on the nightstand beside his bed provided adequate backup security.

Enough light streamed in through curtains the maid had left open to show him the switches on the wall. He flicked them on, flooding the overdone Southwestern decor with light. The garish orange-and-red bedspread leaped out at him. Decorated with bleached cattle skulls, tall saguaro cacti and stick figures that some New York designer probably intended as Kachinas, it was almost as bad as the cheap prints on the wall. The room was clean, however, which was all Harry required.

He closed the curtains and headed for the shower, stripping as he went. Naked, he leaned back against the smooth, slick tiles and let the tepid water sluice over him.

They were close. So damned close. He and Ev had winnowed the thousands of possible combinations of letters and numbers on the postcards down to a hundred or so that made sense. Tomorrow, they'd go over those again, looking for some tie to the local area, some key to a date, a time, a set of coordinates.

They'd worked hard today. Tomorrow, they'd work even harder. The drop had to happen soon. If Paul Gunderson had passed the stuff through Prague four days ago and was triangulating the shipment through Spain and Rio, he had to bring it into the States any day now. Any hour.

Frustration coiled like a living thing in Harry's

gut. Prague. Pamploma. Rio. At last he had a track on the bastard. He wouldn't let him slip through his fingers this time.

He lifted his face to the water, willing himself to relax. He needed to clear his mind, so he could start fresh in a few hours. He needed sleep.

Not that there was much chance of that, he acknowledged, twisting the water off. If last night was any indication, he'd spend half of tonight trying not to think of Sheryl Hancock naked and heavy eyed with pleasure from his kisses, the other half thoroughly enjoying the image.

He slung a towel around his neck and padded into the bedroom. Just as well she had such an amazing memory, he thought grimly. Two days in her company had done enough damage to his concentration. Tomorrow, at least, he wouldn't have to battle the distraction of her smile and her long, endless legs.

Harry almost succeeded in putting both out of his mind. After a short night and a quick breakfast of coffee and *huevos rancheros* in the motel's restaurant, he entered the conference room just after six. Ev arrived at six-thirty, Fay a little later. They slogged through the remaining reports for a couple of hours and had just been joined by an FBI agent with a reputation as an expert in codes and signals when one of the phones rang.

Impatiently, Harry snatched it up. "MacMillan."

"This is Officer Lawrence with the APD. I have a note here to keep you advised of any unusual activity at the Monzano Street post office."

He went still. "Yes?"

"A call came into 911 a few minutes ago, requesting an ambulance at that location."

Ev's desultory conversation with the FBI agent faded into the background. Harry gripped the phone, his eyes fixed on an aeronautical map tacked to the far wall.

"For what reason?"

"I didn't get the whole story. Only that they needed an ambulance to transport a white female to the hospital immediately."

"Did you get a name?"

"No, but I understand it's one of the employees."

His pulse stopped, restarted with a sharp, agonizing kick. "What hospital?"

"University Hospital at UNM."

In one fluid motion, Harry slammed the phone down, shoved back his chair and grabbed his jacket. Throwing a terse explanation over his shoulder to the others, he raced out of the conference room.

Chapter 8

Sheryl called in to work early the next morning to let her supervisor know that Harry had released her from the special task force. Things were quiet for a Friday, Pat Martinez informed her. The temp had her counter station covered, but they could use her help throwing mail on the second shift.

Feeling an unaccountable lack of enthusiasm for a return to her everyday routine, Sheryl decided to run a few errands on her way in. She indulged Button with a supply of doggie treats and herself with a new novel by her favorite romance author before pulling into the parking lot of the Monzano Street station.

The moment she walked through the rear door and headed for the time clock, Sheryl got the immediate impression that things were anything but quiet. Tension hung over the back room, as thick and as heavy as a cloud. The mail carriers who hadn't already started their daily runs crowded around the station supervisor's desk. In the center of the throng, Pat paced back and forth with a phone glued to her ear, her face grave as she spoke to the person on the other end. Peggy, who should have been on the front counter with Elise, was hunched on a corner of Pat's desk. Even Buck Aguilar stood with arms folded and worried lines carved into his usually impassive face.

Sheryl punched in and wove her way through the work stations toward the group clustered around Pat. The station manager's worried voice carried clearly in the silence that gripped her audience.

"Yes, yes, I know. I'll try to reach her again. Just keep us posted, okay?"

The receiver clattered into its cradle.

"They don't know anything yet," she announced to the assembled crowd. "Brian's going to call us as soon as he gets word."

"Brian?" Sheryl nudged her way to the front. "What's Brian going to call about?"

"Sheryl!" Pat sprang up, relief and worry battling on her face. "I've been trying to reach you since right after you called to tell me you were coming in this morning."

"Why? What's going on?"

"Elise fell and went into labor."

"Oh, no!" A tight fist squeezed Sheryl's heart. "Is she okay? And the baby?"

"We don't know. They took her to the hospital by ambulance an hour ago. She was frantic that we get hold of you, since you're her labor coach. I tried your house, then Brian's office, thinking he might know where you were. He didn't, but he went to University Hospital to stay with Elise until we found you."

"Get hold of Brian at the hospital," Sheryl called, already on the run. "Tell him I'll be there in fifteen minutes."

It took her a frustrating, anxious half hour.

She sped down Juan Tabo and swung onto Lomas quickly enough, only to find both westbound lanes blocked by orange barrels. A long line of earthmovers rumbled by, digging up big chunks of concrete. Dust flew everywhere, and Sheryl's anxiety mounted by the second as she waited for the last of them to pass. Even with one lane open each way, traffic crawled at a stop-and-go, five-mile-an-hour pace.

Cursing under her breath, she turned off at the next side street and cut through a sprawl of residential neighborhoods. The Camry's new tires squealed as she slowed to a rolling stop at the stop signs dotting every block, then tore across the intersections. By the time the distinctive dun-colored adobe architecture of the University of New Mexico came into view, she trembled with barely controlled panic.

Elise wasn't due for another two weeks...if then. The baby's sonogram had showed it slightly under-sized, and the obstetrician had revised the due date twice already. With the stress of her divorce coming right on top of the discovery that she was pregnant, Elise hadn't been vague about the possible date of the baby's conception. She and Rick had split up and reconciled twice before finally calling it quits. She could have gotten pregnant during either one of those brief, tempestuous reconciliations.

And Pat had said that Elise had fallen! Every time Sheryl thought of the hard, uncarpeted tile floors at the post office, the giant fist wrapped a little tighter around her heart. Offering up a steady litany of prayers for Elise and her baby, she squealed into the University Hospital parking lot, slammed out of the Camry, and ran for the multistory brown-stucco building.

Since she and Elise had toured the facility as part of their prenatal orientation, she didn't need to consult the directory or ask directions to the birthing rooms. The moment the elevator hummed to a stop on the third floor, she bolted out and ran for the nurses' station in the labor and delivery wing.

"Which room is Mrs. Hart in? Is she all right? I'm her birthing partner—I need to be with her."

A stubby woman in flowered scrubs held up a hand. "Whoa. Slow down and catch your breath. Mrs. Hart's had a rough time, but the hemorrhaging stopped before she went into hard labor."

"Hemorrhaging! Oh, my God!"

"She's okay, really. Last time I checked, she was about to deliver."

"Which room is she in?"

The nurse hesitated. "You'll have to scrub before you can go in, but I'm not sure it's necessary at this point. Her husband's with her. From what I saw a little while ago, he's filling in pretty well as coach."

Sheryl's brows shot up. "Rick's here?"

"I thought he said his name was Brian."

Belatedly, Sheryl remembered the hospital rule restricting attendance in the birthing room during delivery to family members and/or designated coaches.

"We, er, call him 'Rick' for short. Look, I won't burst in, I promise, but I need to be with Elise. Where can I scrub?"

"I'll show you."

A few moments later, a gowned-and-masked Sheryl entered the birthing sanctuary. Doors on either side of the long corridor revealed rooms made homelike by reclining chairs, plants, pictures and low tables littered with magazines. Most of the doors stood open. Two were shut, including Elise's. Mindful of the nurse's injunction, she approached it quietly.

An anguished moan from inside the room raised the hairs on the back of her neck. She nudged the door open an inch or two, and stopped in her tracks.

A trio of medical specialists stood at the foot of the bed, poised to receive the baby. Brian leaned over a groaning, grunting Elise. At least, she thought it was Brian. He was gowned and masked and wearing a surgical cap to keep his auburn hair out of his eyes, and she barely recognized him. She recognized his voice, though, as hoarse and ragged as it was.

"You're doing great. One more push, Elise. One more push."

Sweat glistened on his forehead. His right hand clenched the laboring woman's. With his left, he smoothed her damp hair back from her forehead.

"Breathe with me, then push!"

"I...can't."

"Yes, you can."

"The baby's crowning," the doctor said from the bottom of the bed. "We need a good push here, Mom."

"Breathe, Elise." The command came out in a desperate squeak. Brian swallowed and tried again. "Breathe, then push. Puff. Puff. Puff."

"Puff. Puf...arrrgh!" Elise lifted half off the mattress, then came down with a grunt. Limp and panting, she snarled out a fervent litany.

"Damn Rick! Damn all men! Damn every male who ever learned how to work a zipper!"

Startled, Brian drew back. Elise grabbed the front of his gown and dragged him down to her level.

"Not you! Oh, God, not you! Don't... Don't leave me, Brian. Please, don't leave me."

"I won't, I promise. Now push."

Sheryl peered through the crack in the door, her heart in her throat. After sharing the ups and downs of her friend's divorce and training with her for just this moment, she longed to rush into the room, shove Brian aside and take Elise's hand to help her through the next stage of her ordeal. But her friend's urgent plea and Brian's reply kept her rooted in place. The two of them had bonded. The drama of the baby's imminent birth had forged a link between them that Sheryl couldn't bring herself to break or even intrude on.

"The head's clear," the doctor announced calmly. "Relax a moment, Mom, then we'll work the shoulders. You're doing great. Ready? Okay, here we go."

Sheryl felt her own stomach contract painfully as Elise grunted, then gave a long, rolling moan.

"We've got him."

One of the nurses smiled at the two anxious watchers. "He's a handsome little thing! The spitting image of his dad."

Brian started, then grinned behind his mask. With a whoop of sheer exhilaration, he bent and planted a kiss on Elise's forehead.

She used her death grip on the front of his hospital gown to drag him down even farther. Awkwardly, Brian took her into his arms. She clung to him, sobbing with relief and joy. A second later, the baby gave a lusty wail.

"Don't relax yet," the doctor instructed when Elise collapsed back on the bed, wiped out from her ordeal. "We've still got some work to do here."

Elated, relieved and hugely disappointed that she hadn't participated in the intense drama except as an observer, Sheryl watched Brian smooth back Elise's hair once more. A fierce tenderness came over the part of his face that showed above the mask. The sheer intensity of his expression took Sheryl by surprise. Swiftly, she thought back through the months she and Brian had been dating. She couldn't ever remember seeing him display such raw, naked emotion.

The realization stunned her and added another layer to the wrenching turmoil that had plagued her for two nights now. If she'd had any doubts about the decision she'd made in the dark hours just before dawn this morning, she only needed to look at his face to know it was the right one.

She loved Brian, but she wasn't *in* love with him. Nor, apparently, was he in love with her. Never once had she roused that kind of intense emotion in him. Never had she caused such a display of fierce protectiveness.

Slowly, Sheryl let the door whisper shut and backed away…or tried to. A solid wall of unyielding flesh blocked her way. Turning, she found herself chest to chest with Marshal MacMillan.

"Harry!" She tugged off her face mask. "What are you doing here?"

"I got word that EMS was transporting a female employee from the Monzano Street post office to the hospital. I thought…"

A small muscle worked on one side of his jaw. He paused, then finished in a voice that sounded like glass grinding.

"I thought it might be you."

"Oh, no! Did you think the slasher had come back?"

"Among other things," he admitted, taking Sheryl's elbow to move her to one side as an orderly trundled by with a cart. "By the time EMS verified the patient's identity, I was already in the parking lot, so I came up to see what the problem was."

"Did they tell you? My friend Elise fell and went into labor."

He nodded. "They also told me you were on the way down here, so I waited. How's she doing?"

Sheryl relaxed against the hallway wall, strangely comforted by Harry's presence. "Okay, I think. She and the baby both."

"Good! The nurse said her husband was in with her.

From the glimpse I had over your shoulder a moment ago, he's certainly a proud papa."

"Well, there's a little mix-up about that. Elise is divorced. I was supposed to act as her coach, but I didn't get here in time, so Brian filled in for me."

"Brian?" A puzzled frown flitted across his face. "That was your Brian in there?"

So Harry had seen it, too. The raw emotion. The special bond Brian had forged with Elise.

Sheryl fumbled for an answer other than the one her aching heart supplied. No, he wasn't her Brian. Not any more. Maybe he never had been. But until she talked to him, she wouldn't discuss the matter with anyone else.

Thankfully, one of the nurses walked out of Elise's room at that moment and spared her the necessity of a reply. Sheryl sprang away from the wall and hurried toward her.

"Is everything okay? How are Elise and the baby?"

"Mother and son are both fine," she answered with a smile. "And Dad's so proud, he's about to pop. Give them another few minutes to finish cleaning up, then you can go in."

Their voices must have carried to the occupants of the birthing room, because Brian came charging out a second later. His dark-red hair stuck straight up in spikes. The hospital gown had twisted around his waist. Huge, wet patches darkened his underarms and arrowed down his chest. Sheryl had never seen him looking so ruffled...or so excited.

"Sher! You missed it!" He tore off his mask. "It was

so fantastic! Elise is wonderful. And the baby, he's…
he's wonderful!"

"Yes, I…"

"Look, can you call the school? Elise is worried
about the boys. Tell them I'll pick them up this afternoon and bring them down to see their new brother."

"Sure, I—"

"Thanks! I have to go back in. The doc says it'll be
a few minutes yet before you can come in. You, too…"

He blinked owlishly, as if recognizing for the first
time the man who stood silently behind Sheryl. If Brian
wondered why Harry had turned up at the hospital, he
was too distracted to ask about it now.

"You, too, MacMillan."

He turned away to reenter the birthing room, then
spun back. "You're never going to believe it, Sher! He's
got my hair. Elise's is sort of sorrel, but this little guy
has a cap of dark red fuzz." He grinned idiotically. "Just
like mine."

"Brian!" Sheryl caught him just before he disappeared. "Do you want me to call your office? If you're
going to pick the boys up from school, should I tell
your secretary to reschedule your afternoon appointments?"

He flapped a hand. "Whatever."

The door whirred shut behind him.

"Well, well," Harry murmured in the small, ensuing
silence. "Is that the same man who had to schedule everything, even his meetings with his almost-fiancée?"

"No," Sheryl answered with a sigh. "It isn't."

Turning, she caught a speculative gleam in the

marshal's warm brown eyes. Unwilling to discuss her relationship with Brian until she'd had time to talk to him, she deliberately changed the subject.

"If you want to go in and see Elise and the baby, I'll show you where to find a gown and mask."

"I'd better pass. They don't need a stranger hovering over them right now."

"No, I guess not."

She hesitated, torn between the need to join Elise and a sudden, surging reluctance to say goodbye to Harry for the second time in as many days.

"Thanks for coming down to check on me, even if it wasn't me who needed checking."

"You're welcome."

It took some effort, but she summoned a smile. "Maybe I'll see you around."

The gleam she'd caught in his eyes a moment ago returned, deeper, more intense, like the glint of new-struck gold.

"Maybe you will."

Sheryl spent the rest of the morning and most of the afternoon at the hospital. Brian left after lunch, promising to be back within an hour with Elise's other two boys. His jubilation had subsided in the aftermath of the birth, but his eyes still lit with wonder whenever he caught a glimpse of the baby.

Lazy and at peace in the stillness of the afternoon, Elise cradled her son in her arms and smiled at the woman perched on the edge of her bed. The friend-ship that had stretched across years of shared work and a variety of family crises, big and small, cocooned them.

"I'm sorry you missed your tour of duty as birthing partner, Sher. I could have used your moral support. The others were easy, but I was a little scared with this one after my fall."

"We were all scared."

Elise brushed a finger over the baby's dark-russet down. "I was going to call him Terence, after my grand-father, but I think I'll name him Brian, instead. Brian Hart. How does that sound to you, little one?"

It must have sounded pretty good, as the baby pursed its tiny lips a few times, scrunched its wrinkled face, then settled once more into sleep.

"I don't know what I would have done without Brian," Elise murmured. "He's…wonderful."

Sheryl found a smile. "He says the same thing about you and little Red here."

Her friend's gaze lifted. "I know I've told you this before, but you're so lucky to have him. There aren't many like him around."

"No, there aren't."

Sheryl's smile felt distinctly ragged about the edges. She had to talk to Brian. Soon. This burden of confu-sion and guilt and regret was getting too heavy to lug around much longer.

As it turned out, she didn't have to talk to Brian.

He talked to her.

They met at the hospital later that evening. Elise's room overflowed with flowers and friends from the post office. Murmurs of laughter filled the small room as Peggy and Pat and even Buck Aguilar cooed and showered the new arrival with rattles and blankets and an infant-sized postal service uniform.

Deciding to give the others time and space to admire Baby Brian, Sheryl slipped out and went in search of a vending machine. A cool diet soda fizzed in her hand as she paused by a window, staring out at the golden haze of the sunset.

"Sher?"

She turned and smiled a welcome at Brian. He looked very different from the man who'd rushed out of Elise's room this morning, his face drenched with sweat and his eyes alive with exultation. Tonight, he wore what Sheryl always teasingly called his real-estate-agent's uniform— a lightweight blue seersucker jacket, white shirt, navy slacks. His conservative red tie was neatly knotted.

Leaning against the window alcove, Sheryl offered him a sip of her drink. He declined. His gaze, like hers, drifted to the glorious sunset.

"Have you been in to see Elise and the baby yet?" she asked after a moment.

He nodded. "For a few minutes. I could barely squeeze in the room."

"Did she tell you what she'd decided to name him?"

"Yes."

The single word carried such quiet, glowing pride that Sheryl's heart contracted. God, she hated to hurt this man! They'd shared so many hours, so many dreams. Caught up in her own swamping guilt and regret, she almost missed his next comment.

"I need to talk to you, Sher. I don't know if this is the right time... I don't know if there is a right time." He raked a hand through his hair. "But this morning, when I saw what Elise went through, when I was there with her, I realized what marriage is really about."

Sheryl wanted to weep. She set her drink on the window ledge and took his hands in hers.

"Oh, Brian, I..."

He gripped her fingers. "Let me say this."

"But..."

"Please!"

Miserable beyond words, she nodded.

He took a deep breath and plunged ahead. "Marriage means...should mean...sharing sharing everything. Giving everything. Joining together and, if it's in the picture, holding on to each other at moments like the one that happened this morning."

"I know."

He swallowed, gripping her hands so tightly Sheryl thought her bones would crack. "It shouldn't be something comfortable, something easy and familiar or something we just drift into because it's the next step."

"What?"

His words were so unexpected she was sure she hadn't heard him right.

"Oh, God, Sher, I'm sorry. This hurts so much."

"What does?"

"When I was with Elise this morning, I realized that...that I love you. I'll always love you. But..."

That small "but" rang like a gong in her ears. In growing incredulity, Sheryl stared up at him.

"But what?"

"But maybe… Maybe I don't love you enough," he finished, his eyes anguished. "Maybe not the way a man who might someday stand beside you and hold your hand while you give birth to his children should. I think… I think maybe we shouldn't see each other for a while. Until I sort through this awful confusion, anyway."

Sheryl wouldn't have been human if she'd hadn't experienced a spurt of genuine hurt before her rush of relief. After all, the man she'd spent the better part of the past year with had just dumped her. But she cared for him too much to let him shoulder the entire burden of guilt.

"I love you, too, Brian. I always will. But…"

He went still. "But?"

She gave him a weak, watery smile. "But not in the way a woman who might someday cling to your hand while she gave birth to your children should."

Chapter 9

Sheryl arrived home well after nine that night. Wrung out from the long, traumatic day and her painful discussion with Brian, she dropped her uniform in the basket of dirty clothes that Button, thankfully, had left unmolested.

She thought about crawling into bed. A good cry might shake the awful, empty feeling that had dogged her since she woke up this morning. Arriving at the hospital too late to share the miracle of birth with Elise after all those months of anticipation had only added to her hollowness. The subsequent breakup with Brian had taken that lost feeling to a new low.

As if those disturbing events weren't enough, another lowering realization had hit her as she'd driven home through the dark night. Just twenty-four hours off the task force, and she missed Harry MacMillan as much as she missed her ex-almost.

If not more.

Sighing, Sheryl pulled on a pair of cutoffs and a well-worn pink T-shirt adorned with a covey of road-runners. Try as she might, she couldn't seem to get her mind off the marshal. As soon as he bagged Paul Gunderson, which she sincerely hoped he would soon do, he'd be off after the next fugitive. That was his job. His life. Chances were that she'd never see him again. Utterly depressed by the thought, she scooped Button out of the nest he'd made in the middle of her bed.

"Come on, fella. You're going to keep me company while I sob my way through a schmaltzy movie or two." She knuckled his head around the topknot she'd tied with a red ribbon. "Since I don't have to work tomorrow, we might just make it an all-nighter."

They were halfway through *Ghost,* her all-time favorite tearjerker, when the doorbell rang. Treating Sheryl to an ear-shattering demonstration of newly awakened watchdog instincts, Button dug his claws into her bare thighs and sprang off her lap. Yapping furiously, he raced for the foyer.

Sheryl swiped at her tear-streaked cheeks with the bottom of her T-shirt and followed. To her surprise and instant, bubbling pleasure, she identified Harry MacMillan's unmistakable form through the peephole. Reaching for the door chain, she shouted a command at the dog.

"Quiet!"

Naturally, Button didn't pay the least attention to her. His ear-shattering barks bounced off the walls.

"Will you hush! It's Harry."

She jerked the chain off, flicked the alarm switch and threw open the door. If anything, Button's shrill yips went up a few decibels when he recognized his nemesis, but the marshal had come armed this time. Flashing a grin at Sheryl, he knelt down and wafted a cardboard carton under the dog's nose.

"Like pizza, pug-face? I got double pepperoni for you, pineapple and Canadian bacon for us."

The nerve-shredding barking ceased as if cut off with a knife. To Sheryl's astonishment, Button plopped down on the tiles, rolled all the way over, then scrambled back onto his paws. Jumping up on his hind legs, he danced backward, inviting Harry and the pizza in.

The marshal rose, smirking. "Even hairy little rodents can be bribed. It was just a matter of finding the right price."

Sheryl stood aside, her heart thumping at the crooked grin. "Did you come all the way over here just to bribe your way into Button's good graces?"

"That, and to cheer you up."

Palming the pizza high in the air, he followed her into the apartment. He placed the carton on the whitewashed oak dining table and shrugged out of his jacket. The leather holster followed his sport coat onto the back of a chair. Sheryl turned away from the gun and drank in the sight of Harry's broad shoulders and rugged, tanned face. The smile in his warm brown eyes acted like a balm to her spirits, pulling her out of her depression like a fast-climbing roller coaster.

"What made you think I needed cheering up?" she asked curiously.

"Let's just say my cop's instincts were working overtime again. I also want to go over the info you gave us on the Rio card one more time. Even the FBI's so-called expert can't crack the damned code."

Ahhh. Now the real reason for his visit was out. She didn't mind. Working a few hours with Harry would do her more good than sobbing while Patrick Swayze tried to cross time and space to be with Demi Moore. Or lying in bed, thinking about Brian.

"Have a seat," the marshal instructed, heading for the kitchen. "I think I remember where everything is."

Button trailed at his heels, having abandoned all pride in anticipation of a late-night treat. Sheryl settled into one of the rattan-backed dining-room chairs as instructed and hooked her bare feet on the bottom rung. With a little advance notice of this visit, she might have traded her cutoffs and T-shirt for something more presentable. She might even have pulled a brush through her unruly hair. As it was, Harry would just have to put up with a face scrubbed clean of all makeup and a tumble of loose curls spilling over her shoulders.

He didn't seem to mind her casual attire when he emerged a moment later with plates, napkins and a wineglass filled with the last of the leftover Chablis. In fact, his eyes gleamed appreciatively as his gaze drifted over her.

"I like the roadrunners."

A hint of a flush rose in Sheryl's cheeks. She definitely should have changed…or at least put on a bra under the thin T-shirt.

"We have a lot of them out here," she said primly, then tried to divert his attention from the covey of birds darting across her chest. "Why do you want to go over the Rio card again?"

The glint left his eyes, and his jaw took on a hard angle that Sheryl was coming to recognize.

"I'm missing something. It's probably so simple it's staring me right in the face, but I'll be damned if I can see it."

"Maybe we'll see it tonight."

"I hope so. My gut tells me we're running out of time."

He passed her the wine and plates, then dug in his jacket pocket for a dew-streaked can of beer. The momentary tightness around his mouth eased as he popped the top and hefted the can in the air.

"Shall we toast the baby?"

"Sounds good to me."

Smiling, Sheryl chinked her wineglass against the can. She sipped slowly, her eyes on the strong column of Harry's throat as he satisfied his thirst. For the first time that day, she felt herself relax. Really relax. As much as she could in Harry's presence.

Sure enough, she enjoyed her sense of ease for ten, perhaps twenty, seconds. Then he set his beer on the table, brushed a finger across his mustache and dropped a casual bomb.

"So did you give Brian his walking papers?"

Sheryl choked. Her wineglass hit the whitewashed

oak tabletop with more force than she'd intended. While she fought to clear her throat, Harry calmly served up the pizza.

"Well?"

"No, I didn't give Brian his walking papers! Not that it's any of your business."

"Why not?"

She glared at him across the pizza carton. Getting dumped by Brian was one thing. Telling Harry about it was something else again.

"What makes you think I would even want to?"

He leaned back in his chair, his expression gentle. As gentle as someone with his rugged features could manage, anyway.

"I was there, Sheryl. I saw him with Elise. I also saw your face when he went dashing back into her room."

"Oh."

A small silence spun out between them, broken only by the noisy, snuffling slurps coming from the kitchen. Button, at least, was enjoying his pizza.

Sheryl chipped at the crust with a short, polished nail. She wanted…needed…to talk to someone. Normally, she would have shared her troubled thoughts with Elise. She couldn't burden her friend with this particular problem right now, though, any more than she could call her own mother in Las Cruces to talk about it. Joan Hancock adored Brian, and had told her daughter several thousand times that she'd better latch onto him. Men that reliable, that steady, didn't grow in potato patches.

Maybe… Maybe Harry was just the confidant Sheryl

needed. He knew her situation well enough to murmur sympathetically between slices of pineapple and Canadian bacon, but not so well that he'd burden her with unsolicited advice, as her mother assuredly would.

She stole a glance at him from beneath her lashes. Legs stretched, ankles crossed, he lounged in his chair. He looked so friendly, so relaxed that she couldn't quite believe this was the same man she'd almost taken a bite out of on Inga Gunderson's front porch. His air of easy companionship invited her confidence.

"Brian and I had a long talk tonight in the hospital waiting room," she said slowly. "I didn't give him his walking papers, as you put it. I, uh, didn't get the chance. He gave me mine."

A slice of pizza halted halfway to Harry's mouth. "What?"

"He said that his time with Elise this morning changed every thought, every misconception, he'd ever formed about marriage." She nudged a chunk of pineapple with the tip of her nail. "And about love. It shouldn't be easy, or comfortable, or something we just sort of drift into."

Snorting in derision, the marshal dropped his pizza onto his plate. "No kidding! He's just coming to that brilliant conclusion?"

Sheryl couldn't help smiling at the utter disgust in his voice. Harry MacMillan wouldn't drift into anything. He'd charge in, guns blazing…figuratively, she hoped!

"Don't come down on Brian so hard," she said ruefully. "It took me a while to figure it out, too."

Across the table, golden brown eyes narrowed suddenly. "Are you saying that's all this guy was to you? Someone easy and comfortable?"

"Well…"

The single, hesitant syllable curled Harry's hands into fists. At that moment he would have taken great pleasure in shoving the absent real-estate-agent's face not just into the hallway wall but through it. Hell! It didn't take a Sherlock Holmes, much less a U.S. marshal, to figure out that the jerk hadn't fully committed to Sheryl. If he'd wanted her, really wanted her, he wouldn't have moved so slowly or made any damned appointments! He would've staked his claim with a ring, or at least with a more definitive arrangement than their sort-of engagement.

But after seeing them in each other's arms the other night, Harry had assumed…had thought…

What?

That Sheryl loved the guy? That she wanted Brian Mitchell more than he showed signs of wanting her?

The idea that she might be hurting was what had brought Harry to her apartment tonight. That and the sudden lost look in her eyes when the idiot had rushed back into her friend's hospital room and left her standing there. That look had stayed with Harry all afternoon, until he'd startled Ev and Fay and the FBI expert still struggling with the key words from the postcards by calling it a night. Driven by an urge he hadn't let himself think about, he'd stopped at a pizzeria just a few blocks from Sheryl's apartment and come to comfort her.

He now recognized that urge for what it was. Two parts sympathy for someone struggling with an unraveling relationship: anyone who'd gone through a divorce could relate to that hurt. One part concern for the woman he'd worked with for two days now and had come to like and respect. And one part...

One part pure, unadulterated male lust.

Harry could admit it now. When she'd opened the door to him in those short shorts and figure-hugging T-shirt, a hot spot had ignited in his gut. He knew damned well that the slow burning had nothing to do with any desire to comfort a friend or to grill a team member yet again about the postcards.

It had taken everything he had to return her greeting and nonchalantly set about feeding her and the mutt. He couldn't come anywhere close to nonchalant now, though. Any more than he could keep his gaze from dipping to the thrust of her breasts under the thin layer of pink as she rose and shoved her hands into her back pockets.

"I don't know why I didn't see it sooner, Harry." She paced the open space between the dining and living rooms. "I loved Brian. I still do. But I wasn't *in* love with him. I guess I let myself be seduced by the comfortable routine he represented."

Thoroughly distracted by the sight of those long, tanned legs and bare toes tipped with pink nail polish, Harry forgot his self-assigned role of friend and listener.

"Comfortable routine?" He snorted again. "The man has a helluva seduction technique."

"Hey, it worked for me."

The way she kept springing to Brian's defense was starting to really irritate Harry. Almost as much as her admission that she still loved the jerk.

"Right," he drawled. "That's why you're pacing the floor and ole Bry's off on his own somewhere, pondering the meaning of life and love."

She turned, surprise and indignation sending twin flags of color into her cheeks. "Whose side are you on, anyway?"

"Yours, sweetheart."

He rose, barely noticing the way the endearment slipped out. Three strides took him to where she stood, all stiff and bristly.

"You deserve better than routine, Sheryl. You deserve a dizzy, breathless, thoroughly exhausting seduction that shakes you right out of predictable and puts you down somewhere on the other side of passion."

"Is… Is that right?"

"That's right." He stroked a knuckle down her smooth, golden cheek. "You deserve kisses that wind you up so tight it takes all night to unwind."

Harry could have fallen into the wide green eyes that stared up at him and never found his way out. Her lips opened, closed, opened again. A slow flush stole into her cheeks.

"Yes," she whispered at last. "I do."

Her breasts rose and fell under their pink covering. A pulse pounded at the base of her throat. Slowly, so slowly, her arms lifted and slid around his neck.

"Kiss me, Harry."

He kissed her.

He didn't think twice about it. Didn't listen to any of the alarms that started pinging the instant her arms looped around his neck. Didn't even hear them.

He'd hold her for a moment only, he swore fiercely. Kiss her just once more. Show her that there was life after Brian. That life *with* Brian hadn't come close to living at all. Then his mouth came down on hers, and Sheryl showed him a few things, instead.

That her taste had lingered in his mind for two days. But not this sweet. Or this wild. Or this hot.

That her lips were softer, firmer, more seductive than he remembered.

That her body matched his perfectly. Tall enough that he didn't have to bend double to reach her. Small enough to fit into the cradle of his thighs.

At the contact, he went instantly, achingly, hard. He jerked his head up, knowing that one more breath, one more press of her breasts against his chest, would drive him to something she couldn't be ready for. Not this soon after Brian.

Or maybe she could.

Her eyes opened at his abrupt movement. Harry saw himself in the dark pupils. Saw something else, as well. The passion he'd taunted her about. It shimmered in the green irises. Showed in her heavy eyelids. Sounded in the short, choppy rush of her breath.

This time, she didn't have to ask for his kiss. This time, he gave it, and took everything she offered in return.

By the time she dragged her mouth away, gasping, every muscle in Harry's body strained with the need to press her down on the nearest horizontal surface. With an effort that popped beads of sweat out on his forehead, he loosened his arms enough for her to draw back.

"Harry, I…"

She stopped, swiped her tongue along her lower lip. The burning need in Harry's gut needled into white, hot fingers of fire.

"You what, sweetheart?"

"I want to wind up tight," she whispered, her eyes holding his. "And take all night to unwind."

Few saints would fail to respond to that invitation, and Harry had no illusions that anyone would ever nominate him for canonization. Still, he forced himself to move slowly, giving her time to pull back at any move, any touch.

He lifted a hand to her throat and stroked the smooth skin under her chin. "I think we can manage a little winding and a lot of unwinding. If you're sure?"

A wobbly smile tugged at lips still rosy from his kiss. "Who's being cautious and careful now? What happened to breathless and dizzy and thoroughly exhausting?"

Grinning, he slid his arm under the backs of the thighs that had been driving him insane for the past half hour. Sweeping her into a tight hold, he headed for the hall.

"Breathless and dizzy coming right up, ma'am. Thoroughly exhausting to follow."

Sheryl barely heard Button's startled yip as Harry swept past with her in his arms. She didn't think about the idiocy of what she'd just asked this man to do.

Tomorrow, she'd regret it. Maybe later tonight, when Harry left, as he inevitably would.

At this moment, she wanted only to end the swirling confusion he'd thrown her into the first moment he'd appeared in her life. To get past the pain of her break with Brian. To do something insane, something unplanned and unscheduled and definitely unroutine.

She buried her face in the warm skin of his neck. When he crossed the threshold to her bedroom, he twisted at the waist. With one booted heel, he kicked the door shut behind him. Sharp, annoyed yips rose from the other side.

"I might not hesitate at a little bribery," he told her, his voice a rumble in her ear, "but I draw the line at voyeurism."

"He'll bark all night," Sheryl warned, lifting her head. "Or however long it takes to unwind."

"Let him." His mustache lifted in a wicked grin. "And in case there's any doubt, it's going to take a long time. A very long time."

The husky promise sent ripples of excitement over every inch of her skin. The way he lowered her, sliding her body down his, turned those ripples into a near tidal wave. Her T-shirt snagged on his buttons. It lifted, baring her midriff. Cooled air raised goose bumps above her belly button. Harry's hard, driving kiss raised goose bumps below.

Her shirt hit the floor sometime later. His jeans and boots followed. In a tangle of arms and legs, they tumbled onto the downy black-and-white blanket that covered her bed. Gasping, Sheryl let Harry work the same magic on her breasts that he'd worked on her mouth. His soft, silky mustache teased. His fingers stroked. His tongue tasted. His teeth took her from breathless to moaning to only a kiss or two away from spinning out of control.

Sheryl wasn't exactly a passive participant in her unplanned, unroutine seduction. Her hands roamed as eagerly as his. Her tongue explored. Her body slicked and twisted and pressed everywhere it met his. She was as wet and hot and eager as he was when he finally groaned and dragged her arms down.

"Wait, sweetheart. Wait! Let me get something to protect you."

He rolled off her. Wearing only low-slung briefs and the shirt she'd tugged halfway down his back, he padded across the room to his jeans.

Sheryl flung an arm up over her head, almost as dizzy and befuddled as he'd predicted. Harry's posterior view didn't exactly unfuddle her. Lord, he was magnificent! All long, lean lines. Bronzed muscles. Tight, trim buttocks.

When he scooped up his jeans and turned, she had to admit that his front view wasn't too shabby, either. Her heart hammered as he dug out his wallet and rifled through it with an impatience that fanned the small fires he'd lit under her skin. A moment later, several packages of condoms fell onto the blanket.

Sheryl eyed the abundant supply with a raised brow. Harry caught her look and his mustache tipped into another wicked grin.

"U.S. marshals always come prepared for extended field operations."

"So I see."

Still grinning, he sheathed himself and rejoined her on the bed. He settled between her legs smoothly, as if she were made to receive him. His weight pressed her into the blanket. With both hands, he smoothed her hair back and planted little kisses on her neck.

"I don't want to give you the wrong impression," he murmured against her throat. "Dedicated law enforcement types have all kinds of uses for those little packages."

Torn between curiosity and a wild, blazing need to arch her hips into his, Sheryl could only huff a question into his ear.

"Like…what?"

"Later," he growled, nipping the cords of her neck. "I'll tell you later."

Would they have a later? The brief thought cut through her searing, sensual haze. Then his hand found her core and there was only now. Only Harry. Only the incredible pleasure he gave her.

The pleasure spiraled, spinning tighter and tighter with each kiss, each stroke of his hand and his body. When Sheryl was sure she couldn't stand the whirling sensations a moment longer without shattering, she wrapped her legs around his and arched her hips to receive him. It might have been mere moments or a lifetime later that she exploded in a blaze of white light.

Another forever followed, then Harry thrust into her a final time. Rigid, straining, joined with her at mouth and chest and hip, he filled her body. Only later did she realize that he'd filled the newly empty place in her heart, as well.

The realization came to her as she hovered between boneless satiation and an exhausted doze. Her head cradled on Harry's shoulder, she remembered sleepily that they hadn't gotten around to the postcards. They'd get to them tomorrow, she thought, breathing in the musky scent of their lovemaking.

Tomorrow came crashing down on them far sooner than Sheryl had anticipated. She was sunk in a deep doze, her head still cradled on a warm shoulder, when the sound of a thump and a startled, pain-filled yelp pierced her somnolent semiconsciousness.

Instantly, Harry spun off the bed. Sheryl's head hit the mattress with a thump

"Wh...?"

"Stay here!"

With a pantherlike speed, he dragged on his jeans and yanked at the zipper. They rode low on his hips as he headed for the door. Gasping, Sheryl pushed herself up on one elbow. Still groggy and only half-awake, she blinked owlishly.

"What is it?"

"I don't know, and until I do, stay here, okay? No heroics and no noise."

Before his low instructions had even sunk in, he'd slipped through the door and disappeared into the shadowed hallway. Sheryl gaped at the panel for a second or two, still in a fog. Then she threw back the sheet and leaped out of bed. She had her panties on and her T-shirt half over her head when the door swung open again.

She froze, her heart in her throat.

To her infinite relief, Harry stalked in. Disgust etched in every line of his taut body, he carried a tomato-and-grease-smeared Button under his arm.

"The greedy little beggar climbed up onto the table. He and our half of the pizza just took a dive."

Chapter 10

Although the little heart-shaped crystal clock on her nightstand showed just a few minutes before eleven, by the time Sheryl finished dressing she was experiencing all the awkwardness of a morning-after.

Button's noisy accident had shaken her right out of her sleepy, sensual haze. Like a splash of cold water in her face, reality now set in with a vengeance. She couldn't quite believe she'd begged Harry to kiss her like that. To seduce her, for pity's sake!

She walked down the hall to the living room, cringing inside as she realized how pathetic she must have sounded. First, by admitting that Brian had dumped her. Then, by practically demanding that the marshal take her to bed as a balm to her wounded ego. She couldn't remember when she'd ever done anything so rash. So stupid. So embarrassing to admit to after the fact.

Heat blazed in both cheeks when she found Harry in the dining room. Hunkered down on one knee, he was scrubbing at the grease stains in her carpet with a sponge and muttering imprecations at the dog that sat a few feet away, watching him with a show of blasé interest.

"You don't have to do that," Sheryl protested, her discomfiture mounting at the sight of Harry's naked chest. Had she really wrapped her arms and legs and everything else she could around his lean, powerful torso?

She had, she admitted with a new flush of heat. She could still feel the ache in her thighs, and taste him on her lips. How in the world had she lost herself like that? She hardly knew much more about this man than his name, his occupation, his marital status and the fact that he logged more travel miles in a month than most people did in two years. That alone should have stopped her from throwing herself at him the way she had! Hadn't she learned her lesson from her parents?

Obviously not. Even now, she ached to wrap her arms around him once again. Smart, Sheryl! Real smart. Dropping to her knees, she reached for the sponge.

"I'll do that while you get dressed."

He looped an arm across his bent knee and regarded her with a lazy smile.

"Unwound already, Sher? And here I promised that it would take all night."

His teasing raised the heat in her cheeks to a raging inferno. She attacked the pizza stain, unable to meet his eyes.

"Yes, well, I know you came here to work, not to, uh, help me get past this bad patch with Brian, and you don't have all night for that."

His hand closed over her wrist, stilling her agitated movements. When she looked up, his air of lazy amusement had completely disappeared.

"Is that what you think just happened here? That I played some kind of sexual Good Samaritan by taking you to bed?"

She wouldn't have put it in quite those words, but she couldn't deny the fact that he'd done exactly that.

"Don't think that I'm not..." She swallowed. "That I'm not grateful. I needed a...a distraction tonight and you—"

With a swiftness that made her gasp, he rose, bringing her up with him. Sudden, fierce anger blazed in his brown eyes.

"A distraction?" he echoed in a tone that raised the fine hairs on the back of her neck. "You needed a distraction?"

Sheryl knew she was digging herself in deeper with every word, but she didn't have the faintest idea how to get out of this hole. She'd only wanted to let Harry know that she didn't expect him to continue the admittedly spectacular lovemaking she'd forced on him. Instead, she'd unintentionally ruffled his male ego. More embarrassed than ever, she tugged her wrist free.

"That didn't come out the way I meant it. You were more than a distraction. You were..." Her face flaming, she admitted the unvarnished truth. "You were wonderful. Thank you."

Harry stared at her, at a total loss for words for one of the few times in his life. Anger still pounded through him. Incredulity now added its own sideswiping kick. He couldn't believe that Sheryl had just *thanked* him, for God's sake! If this whole conversation didn't make him so damned furious, he might have laughed at the irony of it. He couldn't remember the last time he'd lost himself so completely, so passionately, in a woman's arms. Or the last time he'd drifted into sleep with a head nestled on his shoulder and a soft, breathy sigh warming his neck.

Harry hadn't exactly sworn off female companionship in the years since his divorce, but neither had he ignored the lessons he'd learned from that sobering experience. As long as he made his living chasing renegades, he couldn't expect any woman to put up with his here-today, gone-tonight lifestyle. Deliberately, he'd kept his friendships with women light and casual. Even more deliberately, he dated women whose own careers or interests coincided with the transitory nature of his. In any case, he sure as hell had never jeopardized an ongoing investigation by seducing one of the key players involved.

He'd broken every one of his self-imposed rules tonight. Deep in his gut, Harry knew damned well that he'd break them again if Sheryl turned her face up to his at this moment and asked him in that sweet, seductive way of hers to kiss her. Hell, he didn't need asking. Wide-awake now and still tight from the crash that had brought him springing out of bed, he had to battle the urge to sweep Sheryl into his arms and take her back to bed to show her just how much of a *distraction* he could provide. Just the thought of burying himself in her slick, satiny heat once again sent a spear of razor-sharp need through him.

With something of a shock, Harry realized that he wanted this woman even more fiercely now than he had before she'd given herself to him. And here she was, brushing him off with a polite thank-you.

Despite her red cheeks, she met his gaze with a dignity that tugged at something inside him. Something sharper than need. Deeper than desire.

"I'm sorry," she said quietly. "I didn't mean to insult you or cheapen what happened between us. It *was* wonderful, Harry. I just didn't want you to think that I want…or expect…anything more. I know why you're in Albuquerque, and that you'll be gone as soon as something breaks on your fugitive."

She had just put his own thoughts into words. Harry didn't particularly like hearing them.

"Sheryl…"

Her eyes gentled. Her hand came up to stroke his cheek. "It's all right, Marshal. Some men are wanderers by nature as much as by profession. My father was one. So, I think, are you. I understand."

Harry wasn't sure he did. He heard what she was saying. He agreed with it completely. So why did he want to—

The muted shrill of his cellular phone interrupted his chaotic thoughts. Frowning, he extracted the instrument from the jacket he'd left hanging on the back of a dining-room chair.

"MacMillan."

"Harry!" Ev's voice leaped out at him. "Where the hell are you?"

"At Sheryl's apartment." He didn't give his partner a chance to comment on that one. "Where are you?"

"Outside your motel room. I was on my way home when I got the news. I swung by your place to give you the word personally."

"What word?"

"The Santa Fe airport manager just called. He's got a small, twin-engine jet about two hours out, requesting permission to land."

Harry's gut knotted. "And?"

"And the pilot also requested that Customs be notified. He wants to off-load a cargo of Peruvian sheepskin hides destined for a factory just outside Taos that manufactures those Marlboro-man sheepskin coats. From what I'm told, the hides stink. Like you wouldn't believe. Customs isn't too happy about processing the cargo tonight."

"This could be it," his listener said softly.

"I think it is. The FAA ran a quick check on the aircraft's tail number and flight plan. This leg of the flight originated in Peru, but the aircraft is registered in Brazil, Harry. Brazil!"

"Get a helo warmed up and ready for us."

"Already done. It's on the pad at State Police headquarters. Fay's on her way there now."

"I'll meet you both in ten minutes."

Harry snapped the phone shut and jammed it into his jacket. Every sense, every instinct, pushed at him to race into the bedroom and grab his clothes. To slam out of the apartment, jump into his car and hit the street, siren wailing.

For the first time that he could remember, his cop's instincts took second place to a stronger, even more urgent demand. In answer to the question in Sheryl's wide eyes, he paused long enough to give her a swift recap.

"We've got a break, Sher. A plane registered in Brazil is coming into the Santa Fe airport in a couple of hours."

"No kidding!"

She was still standing where he'd left her when he came running back, shoving his shirttail into his jeans. He grabbed his holster and slipped into it with a roll of his shoulders. Then he snatched up his jacket and strode to where she stood. His big hands framed her face.

"I've got to go."

"I know. Be careful."

He gave himself another second to sear her eyes and her nose and the tangled silk of her hair into his memory. Then he kissed her, hard, and headed for the door.

"Harry!"

"What?"

"Come back when you can. I, uh, want to know what happens."

"I will."

The nondescript government sedan squealed out of the apartment complex. With one eye on the late-night traffic, Harry fumbled the detachable Kojak light into its mounting and flipped its switch. The rotating light slashed through the night like a sword. A half second later, he activated the siren and shoved the accelerator to the floor. The unmarked, unremarkable vehicle roared to life.

Ten minutes later, the car squealed through the gates leading to the headquarters of Troop R of the New Mexico Highway Patrol. Grabbing the duffel bag containing his field gear from the trunk, Harry raced for the helo pad. Ev and Fay met him halfway, both jubilant, both lugging their own field gear.

"Give me a rundown on who we've got playing so far," Harry shouted over the piercing whine of the helicopter's engine.

"Our Santa Fe highway patrol detachment is pulling in every trooper they've got to cordon off the airport," Fay yelled. "The Santa Fe city police have alerted their SWAT team. They'll be in place when we get there."

They ducked under the whirring rotor blades and climbed aboard through the side hatch. The copilot greeted them with a grin and directed them to the web rack that stretched behind the operators' seats.

Panting, Ev buckled himself in. "Customs has a Cessna Citation in the air tracking our boy as we speak. They've also got two Blackhawks en route from El Paso, with a four-man bust team aboard each."

Fierce satisfaction shot through Harry at the news. The huge Sikorsky UH-60 Blackhawk helicopters came equipped with an arsenal of lethal weapons and enough candlepower to light up half of New Mexico.

"Good. We might just give them a chance to show their stuff."

While the copilot buckled himself in, the pilot

stretched around to show the passengers where to plug in their headsets.

"What's the flying time to Santa Fe?" Harry asked, his words tinny over the static of the radio.

"Twenty minutes, sir."

"Right. Let's do it."

The aviator gave him a thumbs-up and turned her attention to the controls. Seconds later, the chopper lifted off. It banked steeply, then zoomed north.

Harry used the short flight to coordinate the operation with the key players involved. The copilot patched him through to the Customs National Aviation Center in Oklahoma City, which was now tracking the suspect aircraft, the New Mexico state police ops center and the Santa Fe airport manager.

"Our boy is still over an hour out." he summarized for Ev and Fay. "That gives us plenty of time to familiarize ourselves with the layout of the field and get our people into position. No one moves until I give the signal. No one. Understood?"

Harry didn't want any mistakes. No John Waynes charging in ahead of the cavalry. No hotshot Rambos trying to show their stuff. If the man he'd been tracking for almost a year was flying in aboard this aircraft, the bastard wasn't going to get away. Not this time.

The short flight passed in a blur of dark mountains to their right and the sparse lights of the homes scattered along the Rio Grande valley below. The helo set down at the Santa Fe airport just long enough for Harry and the two others to jump out. Bent double, they dashed through the cloud of dust thrown up by the rotor wash.

As soon as they were clear, Harry shed his coat and pulled his body armor out of his gear bag. A dark, lightweight windbreaker with "U.S. Marshal" emblazoned on the back covered the armor and identified him to the other players involved. After shoving spare ammo clips into his pockets, he checked his weapon, then went to meet the nervous airport manager waiting for him inside the distinctive New Mexico-style airport facility.

In a deliberate attempt to retain Santa Fe's unique character and limit its growth, the city planners had also limited the size of the airport that serviced it. To make access even more difficult, high mountain peaks ringed its relatively short runway. Consequently, no large-bodied jetliners landed in the city. The millions of tourists a year who poured into Santa Fe from all over the world usually flew into Albuquerque and drove the fifty-five-mile scenic route north. Even the legislators who routinely traveled to the capital to conduct their business did so by car or by small aircraft.

The inconvenient access might have constituted an annoyance for some travelers, but it added up to a major plus for Harry and the team members who gathered within minutes of his arrival. With only one north-south runway and the parallel taxiway to cover, he quickly orchestrated the disposition of his forces. They melted into the night like dark shadows, radios muted and lights doused.

After a final visual and radar check of their handheld secure radios, Ev headed for the tower to coordinate the final approach and takedown. Harry and Fay climbed into the airport service vehicle that would serve as their mobile command post. When the truck pulled into its customary slot beside the central hangar, Harry stared into the night.

A million stars dotted the sky above the solid blackness of the mountains. Richard Johnson, aka Paul Gunderson, was out there somewhere. With any luck, that somewhere would soon narrow down to a stretch of runway in the high New Mexico desert.

A shiver rippled along Harry's spine, part primal anticipation, part plain old-fashioned chill. Even in mid-June, Sante Fe's seven-thousand-foot elevation put a nip in the night air. He zipped his jacket, folded his arms. His eyes on the splatter of stars to the south, the hunter settled down to await his prey.

The minutes crawled by.

The secure radio cackled as Ev gave periodic updates on the aircraft's approach. Forty minutes out. Thirty. Twenty.

The Blackhawks swept over the airport, rotors thumping in the night, and touched down behind the hangars. One would move into position to block any possible takeoff attempt should anything spook the quarry once it was on the ground. The second would come in from the rear.

Quiet settled over the waiting, watching team. Even Ev's status reports were hushed.

Fifteen minutes.

Ten.

This was for Dean, Harry promised the dark, silent night. For the man who'd razzed him as a rookie, and stood beside him at the altar, and asked him to act as godfather to his son. And for Jenny, who'd cried in Harry's arms until she had no more tears left to shed. For every marshal who'd ever died in the line of duty, and every son or mother or husband or wife left behind.

Without warning, an image of Sheryl formed in Harry's mind. Her hair tumbling around her shoulders. Her eyes wide with excitement and the first, faint hint of worry on his behalf. It struck him that he'd left Sheryl, as Dean had left Jenny, to chase after Paul Gunderson.

Dean had never returned.

Harry might not, either. Dammit, he shouldn't have made that rash promise to Sheryl. Even without the hazards inherent in his job, success bred its own demands. If Gunderson stepped off an airplane in Santa Fe in the next few minutes, as Harry sincerely prayed he would, he'd climb right back on a plane, this time in handcuffs and leg irons. Harry would go with him. He wouldn't be driving back to Sheryl's place to give her a play-by-play of the night's events…or to redeem the promise of the hard, swift kiss he'd left her with.

He had no business making her any kind of promises at all, he thought soberly.

Even if he wanted to, he couldn't offer her much more than a choice between short bursts of pleasure and long stretches of loneliness. And a husband whose job might or might not leave her weeping in someone's arms, as Dean's had left Jenny.

Suddenly, the radio cackled. "He's on final approach. Check out that spot of light at one o'clock, 'bout two thousand feet up."

Harry blanked his mind of Sheryl, of Jenny, even of Dean. His eyes narrowed on the tiny speck of light slowly dropping out of the sky.

The takedown was a textbook operation.

Following the tower's directions, the twin-engine King Air rolled to a stop on the parking apron, fifty yards from where Harry waited in the service vehicle. As soon as the engines whined down and the hatch opened, the Blackhawks rose from behind the adjacent hangar like huge specters. They dropped down, their thirty-million-candlepower spotlights pinning the two figures who emerged from the King Air in a blinding haze of white light. The helo crews poured out.

Harry clicked the mike on the vehicle's loudspeaker and shouted a warning. "This is the U.S. Marshals Service. Hit the ground. Now!" He was out of the vehicle, his weapon drawn, before the echoes had stopped bouncing off the hangar walls.

The two figures took one look at the dark-suited figures converging on them from all directions and dropped like stones.

Harry reached them as they hit the pavement. Disappointment rose like bile in his throat. Even from the back, he could see that neither of the individuals spread-eagled on the concrete fit Paul Gunderson's physical description.

Ev Sloan reached the same conclusion when he panted up beside Harry a moment later.

"He's not with 'em. Damn!"

"My sentiments exactly," Harry got out through

clenched jaws. Raising his voice, he issued a curt order. "All right. On your feet. We need to inspect your cargo."

A two-man Customs team went through the King Air's cargo with dogs, handheld scanners and an array of sophisticated chemical testing compounds. A second team searched the plane itself, which had been towed into a hangar for privacy.

By the time the first streaks of a golden dawn pierced the darkness of the mountain peaks outside, unbaled sheepskin hides lay strewn along one half of the hangar. Barely cured and still wearing a coat of gray, greasy wool, they gave off a stench that had emptied the contents of several team members' stomachs and put the drug dogs completely out of action.

The plane's guts lay on the other side of the hangar floor…along with a neat row of plastic bags. Even without the dogs, the stash in the concealed compartment in the plane's belly had been hard to miss.

The senior Customs agent approached Harry, grinning. Sweat streaked his face, and he carried the stink of hides with him.

"Five hundred kilos and a nice, new King Air for the Treasury Department to auction off. Not a bad haul, Marshal. Not bad at all."

"No. Just not the one we wanted."

The agent thrust out his hand. "Sorry you didn't get your man this time. Maybe next time."

"Yeah. Next time."

Leaving the other agency operatives to their prizes, Harry walked out into the slowly gathering dawn. Ev leaned against the hood of a black-and-white state police car, sipping coffee from a leaking paper cup. Then he tossed out the dregs of his coffee and crumpled the cup.

"Well, I guess it's back to the damned computer printouts and postcards. You get anything more from Sheryl when you were up at her place last night?"

"No."

And yes.

Harry had gotten far more from her than he'd planned or hoped for. The need to return to her apartment, to finish this damnable night in her arms, tore through his layers of weariness.

He thought of a thousand reasons why he shouldn't go back…and one consuming reason why he should.

Chapter 11

Sheryl curled in a loose ball on top of the black-and-white blanket. Button lay sprawled beside her. She stroked his silky fur with a slow, light touch, taking care not to wake him while he snuffled and twitched in the throes of some doggie dream. Her gaze drifted to the small crystal clock on the table beside her bed.

Five past six.

Seven hours since Harry had left. Seven hours of waiting and worrying. Of wondering when...if...he'd come back. He'd been gone for only seven hours, yet it seemed as though days had passed since he'd rolled out of this bed and raced into the kitchen in response to Button's attack on the pizza.

Until tonight, Sheryl had never really appreciated the loneliness that had turned her mother into such a bitter, unhappy woman. She'd seen it happening, of course. Even as a child, she'd recognized that her father's extended absences had leached the youth from her mother's face and carved those small, tight lines on either side of her face. Mentally, she'd braced herself every time her father walked out the door. She'd shared her mother's hurt and dissatisfaction, but she'd never *felt* the emptiness deep inside her, as she had these past hours. Never experienced this sense of being so alone.

Despite the hollow feeling in her chest, Sheryl could summon no trace of bitterness. Instead of hurt, a lingering wonder spread through her veins every time she thought of the hours together with Harry. Her breasts still tingled from his stinging kisses. One shoulder still carried a little red mark from his prickly mustache. She'd never experienced anything even remotely resembling the explosions of heat and light and skyrocketing sensation the marshal had detonated under her skin. Not once but twice.

Recalling her fumbling attempt to thank him for services rendered, Sheryl almost groaned aloud. Talk about putting her foot in it! Harry had bristled all over with male indignation. For a moment, he'd looked remarkably like Button with his fur up.

Smiling, she combed her fingers through the soft, feathery ruff decorating the paw closest to her. The shih tzu snuffled and jerked his leg away. One black eye opened and glared at her though the light of the gathering dawn.

"Sorry."

He gave a long-suffering look and rolled onto his back, all four paws sticking straight up in the air. Sheryl speared another glance at the clock. Six-fifteen.

Too restless to even pretend sleep any longer, she tickled the dog's pink belly. "Want to get up? You can finish off the pizza for breakfast."

Black gums pulled back. A warning growl rumbled up from the furry chest. Hastily, Sheryl pulled her fingers out of reach.

"Okay, okay! You don't mind if I get up, do you?"

Silly question. Before she'd was halfway across the bedroom, Button was already sunk back into sleep.

A quick shower washed away the grittiness of her sleepless night. Since it was Saturday, Sheryl didn't even glance at the uniforms hanging neatly in her closet. Instead, she pulled out her favorite denim sundress. With its thin straps, scooped neck and loose fit, it was perfect for Albuquerque's June heat. Tiny wooden buttons marched down the front and stopped above the knee, baring a long length of leg when she walked. The stone-washed blue complemented her tan and her streaky blond hair, she knew. Now all she had to do was erase the signs of her sleepless night. Making a face at her reflection in the mirror, she applied a little blush and a swipe of lipstick. A few determined strokes with the brush subdued her hair into a semblance of order. Clipping it back with a wooden barrette that matched the buttons on the dress, she padded barefoot into the kitchen.

The first thing she saw was the pizza carton on the counter. Instantly, she started worrying and wondering again.

Where was Harry? What had happened after he'd left her last night?

Leaning a hip against the counter, she filled the automatic coffeemaker and waited while it brewed. Slowly, a rich aroma spread through the kitchen. Even more slowly, the soft, golden dawn lightened to day.

The sound of Button's nails clicking on the tiles alerted her to the fact that he'd decided to join the living. He wandered into the kitchen and gave her a disgruntled look, obviously as annoyed with her early rising as he'd been with her tossing and turning.

"Do you need to go out? Hold on a sec. I'll get the paper and pour a cup of coffee and join you on the back patio."

Sheryl flicked off the alarm and went outside to hunt down her newspaper. As usual, the deliveryman had tossed it halfway across the courtyard. She didn't realize Button had slipped out the front door with her until his piercing yip cut through the early morning quiet.

Startled, Sheryl spun around. From the corner of one eye, she saw Button charge across the courtyard toward the silver-haired Persian that had been sunning itself at the base of the small fountain. The cat went straight up in the air, hissing, and came down with claws extended.

"Oh, no!"

Oblivious to her dismayed exclamation, Button leaped to attack. His quarry decided that discretion was the better part of valor. Streaking across the tiled courtyard, it disappeared through the arched entryway that led to the parking lot. The shih tzu followed in noisy pursuit.

The darned dog was going to wake every person in the apartment complex with that shrill bark. Dropping the paper, Sheryl joined in the chase.

"Button! Here, boy! Here!"

She rounded the entryway corner just in time to see both cat and dog dart across the parking lot. Another cluster of apartments swallowed them up. Sheryl started across the rough asphalt. Suddenly, her bare heel came down on a pebble. Pain shot all the way up to the back of her knee.

"Dammit!"

Wincing, she took a few limping steps, then ran awkwardly on the ball of her injured foot. To her consternation, the noisy barking grew fainter and fainter. A moment later, it disappeared completely, swallowed up by the twisting walkways, picturesque courtyards and multistory buildings of the sprawling complex.

Seriously concerned now, Sheryl ran through archway after archway. Button would never find his way back through this maze. Stepping up the pace as much as the pain in her heel would allow, she searched the apartment grounds. Her dress skirt flapped around her knees. The wooden barrette holding her hair back snapped open and clattered to the walkway behind her. Sweat popped out on her forehead and upper lip.

"Button!" she called in gathering desperation. "Here, boy! Come to Sheryl!"

Her breath cut through her lungs like razor blades when she caught the sound of a crash, followed by a yelp. She tore down another path and through an archway, then came to a skidding, one-heeled halt. If she'd had any breath left, Sheryl would have gasped at the scene that greeted her. As it was, she could only pant helplessly.

An oversized clay pot had been knocked on its side. It now spilled dirt and pink geraniums onto the tiles. Beside the overturned pot lay a tipped-over sundial. Colorful fliers and sections of a newspaper littered the courtyard. In the midst of the havoc, not one but two silver Persians now stood shoulder to shoulder. Fur up, backs arched, they hissed for all they were worth. Their indignant owner stood behind them, flapping her arms furiously at the intruder. Button was belly to the ground, but hadn't given up the fight.

By the time Sheryl had scooped up the snarling shih tzu, apologized profusely to the cats' owner, offered to pay for the damages and listened to an irate discourse on dog owners who ignore leash laws, the sun had tipped over the apartment walls and heated the morning. Limping and hot and not exactly happy with her unre- pentant houseguest, she lectured him sternly as she retraced her steps to her apartment. She took a wrong turn twice, which didn't improve her mood or Button's standing. Unconcerned over the fact that he was in disgrace, the dog surveyed the areas they passed through, ears up and eyes alert for his next quarry.

Sheryl was still lecturing when she rounded the corner of her building. The sight of two squad cars pulled up close to the arch leading to her courtyard stopped her in midscold. Curious and now a little worried, she hurried through the curving entrance. Worry turned to gulping alarm when she saw a uniformed officer standing just outside her open apartment door.

Oh, God! Something must have gone wrong last night! Maybe Harry was hurt!

Her heart squeezed tight. So did her arms, eliciting an indignant squawk from Button.

"Sorry!"

Easing the pressure on the little dog, she ran across the courtyard. "What's going on? What's happened?"

"Miss Hancock?"

"Yes. Is Harry all right?"

"Harry?"

"Harry MacMillan. Marshal MacMillan."

"Oh, yeah. He's inside. He's the one who called us when he found your front door open."

Sheryl fought down an instant rush of guilt. She'd forgotten all about the security systems in her worry over Button.

"Are you all right, Miss Hancock?"

"Yes, I'm fine."

"Then where the hell have you been?"

The snarl spun Sheryl around. Harry filled her doorway, his body taut with tension and his eyes furious. Another uniformed police officer hovered at his shoulder.

She took one look at his face and decided this wasn't the time to tell him about the wild chase Button had led her through the apartment complex. In the mood he was obviously in, he'd probably skin the dog whole.

"I, uh, went out to get the newspaper."

His blistering look raked her from her sweat-streaked face to her bare toes, then moved to the rolled newspaper lying a few yards away…right where Sheryl had dropped it.

"You want to run that by me one more time?"

She didn't care for his tone. Nor did she appreciate being dressed down like a recruit in front of the two police officers.

"Not particularly."

Although she wouldn't have thought it possible, his jaw tightened another notch. Turning to the police officer, he held out a hand.

"Looks like I called you out on a false alarm. Sorry."

"No problem, Marshal."

"Thanks for responding so quickly."

"Anytime."

With a nod to Sheryl and Button, the two policemen departed the scene. Harry turned to face her, his temper still obviously simmering. In no mood for a public fracas, Sheryl brushed past him and headed for the cool sanctuary of her apartment.

Harry trailed after her, scowling. "Why are you limping?"

"I stepped on a stone."

For some reason, that seemed to incense him even further. He followed her inside, lecturing her with a lot less restraint than she'd lectured Button just a few moments ago.

"That could have been glass you stepped on."

"Well, it wasn't."

"Running around barefoot is about as smart as leaving your front door wide-open! Speaking of which…"

The oak door slammed behind her, rattling the colorful Piña prints on the entryway wall.

"You want to tell me what good a security system is if you don't even bother to close the damned door?"

Enough was enough. Sheryl had run a good mile or more after the blasted mutt. She was hot and sweaty. Her hair hung in limp tendrils around her face. Her heel still hurt like hell. And she'd spent most of the night worrying about a U.S. marshal who, judging from his foul temper, obviously hadn't apprehended the fugitive he wanted.

Bending, she released the dog. Button promptly scampered off, leaving her to face the irate Harry on her own. She turned to find him standing close. Too close. She could see the stubble darkening his cheeks and chin…and the anger still simmering in his whiskey-gold eyes.

Drawing in a deep breath, she decided to go right to the source of that anger. "I take it Paul Gunderson wasn't aboard the plane you intercepted."

"No, he wasn't."

"I'm sorry."

"Yeah," he rasped. "Me, too. And it didn't exactly help matters when I arrived to find your apartment wide-open and you gone."

"Okay, that was careless."

"Careless? How about idiotic? Irresponsible?

"How about we don't get carried away here?" she snapped back.

Her spurt of defiance seemed to fuel his anger. He stepped even closer. Sheryl refused to back away, not that she could have if she'd wanted to. Her shoulder blades almost pressed against the wall as it was.

"Do you have any idea what I went through when I found the door open and you missing?"

The savagery in his voice jolted through her like an

electrical shock. In another man, the suppressed violence might have frightened her. In Harry, it thrilled the tiny, adventurous corner of her soul she'd never known she possessed until he'd burst into her life.

How could she have fooled herself into believing she wanted safe and secure and comfortable? The truth hit her with devastating certainty.

She wanted the fierce emotion she saw blazing in this man's eyes.

She wanted the fire and excitement and the passion that only he had stirred in her.

She wanted Harry…however she could have him.

"No," she whispered. "I don't know what you went through. Tell me."

He buried his hands in her hair and pulled her head back. "I'll show you."

This kiss didn't even come close to resembling the ones they'd shared last night. Those were wild and tender and passionate. This one was raw. Elemental. Primitive. So powerful that Sheryl's head went back and her entire body arched into his.

Nor did Harry display any of the teasing finesse he'd used on her before. His mouth claimed hers. Rough and urgent, his hands found her hips and lifted her into him. Sweat-slick and breathless and instantly aroused, Sheryl felt him harden against her.

He dragged his head up. Nostrils flaring, he stared down at her. Raw male need stretched the skin over his cheekbones tight and turned the golden lights in his eyes to small, blazing fires.

Sheryl wasn't stupid. She knew that this barely controlled savagery sprang as much from his frustration over his failure to nab Paul Gunderson last night as from the worry and anger she'd inadvertently sparked in him this morning. She didn't care. Wherever it sprang from, it consumed her.

Wanting him every bit as fiercely as he wanted her, she slid an arm around his neck and dragged his head back down. She knew the instant his mouth covered hers that a kiss wasn't enough. She fumbled for his belt buckle. He stiffened, then attacked the wooden buttons on her denim sundress. The little fasteners went flying. They landed on the tiles with a series of sharp pops. The dress hit the floor somewhere between the entryway and the bedroom. His jeans and shirt followed.

On fire with a need that slicked her inside and out, Sheryl pushed Harry to the bed and straddled him. He was ready for her. More than ready. But when he reached for her hips to lift her onto his rigid shaft, she wiggled backward.

"Oh, no! Not this time. This time, I want to give you what you gave me last night."

"Sheryl…"

"I'm going to wind you up tight," she promised. "And leave you breathless and dizzy and wanting more."

Much more. So much more.

Her fingers combed the hair on his belly. Moved lower. At her touch, his stomach hollowed. Hot, velvety steel filled her hand. Sheryl's throat went dry. She ran her tongue over her lips.

His shaft leaped in her hand. With a wicked smile

that surprised her almost as much as it did Harry, she bent and proceeded to leave him breathless and groaning and wanting more.

Much more.

She was still smiling when she and Harry both dropped into an exhausted stupor.

A bounce of the bedsprings woke her with a jerk some time later. Harry shot straight up, his face a study in sleep-hazed confusion.

"Oh, God!" she moaned. "What now?"

"Did you just—"

He broke off, his entire body stiffening. An expression of profound disgust replaced his confusion. Yanking back the rumpled black-and-white Zuni blanket, he glared at the animal wedged comfortably between their knees.

Button lifted his head and snarled, obviously as displeased at having his rest disturbed as Harry was. The two males wore such identical expressions of dislike that Sheryl fell back on the bed, giggling helplessly.

"You should see your face," she gasped.

Harry didn't share her amusement. "Yeah, well, you should try waking up to a set of claws raking down your thigh."

"I have," she told him, still giggling. "Believe me, I have."

For a moment, he looked as though he intended to take Button on for undisputed possession of the bed. Bit by bit, the light of battle went out of his eyes. Rasping a hand across his chin, he let out a long breath.

"I've got to go."

Sheryl's giggles died, but she managed to keep her smile going. "I know."

"Even though we didn't get Gunderson, we've still got some matters to clear up from last night. Ev will be waiting for me."

She nodded.

"Mind if I use your shower?"

"Be my guest," she said with deliberate nonchalance. "I've even got a razor in there. It's contoured for a woman's legs, but I think it'll scrape off everything but your mustache."

While the water pelted against the shower door, Sheryl slipped out of bed and retrieved her sundress. She wouldn't regret his leaving, she repeated over and over, as if it were a mantra. She wouldn't try to hold him.

She couldn't, even if she wanted to.

She could only keep her smile fixed firmly in place when he walked out of the shower, his chest bare above his jeans and his dark hair glistening.

He gathered his clothes. By the time he buckled on his holster, a frown creased his brow. He crossed to where she sat on the edge of the bed.

"I'll call you."

"Ha! That's what they all say."

Her feeble attempt at humor fell flat. If anything, the line in his forehead grooved even deeper.

"I'll call you. That's all I can promise."

Sheryl sympathized with the wrenching conflict she saw in his eyes. He wanted to leave. Needed to leave.

Yet something he couldn't quite articulate tugged at him. That something gave her the courage to rise slowly and lift her palms to his cheeks.

Like Harry, she'd gone through a bit of wrenching herself in the past few days. Without wanting to, without trying to, she'd slipped out of her nice, easy routine and discovered that she wanted more of life than comfort and security.

Harry had shown her what life could…should…be. He'd given her a taste of excitement, of adventure. Of something that she was beginning to recognize as love. She wasn't sure when she'd fallen for this rough-edged marshal, but she had. She suspected it had happened last night, when she'd opened the door and found him standing there with his pineapple-and-Canadian-bacon pizza. She'd known it this morning, when he pinned her against the wall and everything inside her had leaped at his touch.

She was willing to take a chance that what she felt could withstand the test of time. The trial of separation and the tears of loneliness. She wanted to believe that what she could share with Harry was special, different…unlike what her parents had shared.

He hadn't reached that point yet. She saw the hesitation in his eyes. Heard it in his voice. Maybe he'd never reach it. Maybe he'd walk out the door, get caught up in his investigation and forget her.

And maybe he wouldn't.

Sheryl would risk it.

"I didn't ask for any promises, Marshal," she said softly. "I don't need them."

Her smile gentling, she rose on tiptoe and brushed his mouth with a kiss.

"Call me when you can."

For the next few hours, she jumped every time the phone rang…which didn't make for a restful morning, considering that it rang constantly.

Elise called first. After a glowing recount of the baby's first night, she mentioned that the doctor had cleared them both to go home tomorrow.

"So soon?"

"It'll be forty-eight hours, Sher. That's long enough for either of us."

"I'll drive you."

"Thanks, but Brian said he would take us home. Do you suppose you could swing by my house to pick up some clean clothes, though? Mine got a little messed up when I fell."

"Sure." Wedging the phone between her ear and her shoulder, Sheryl reached for a pad and pen. "Tell me what you need."

She scribbled down the short list and hung up, promising to see Elise and the baby later this morning. Just seconds after that, the phone rang again. Her heart jumping, she snatched up the receiver.

It took some doing, but she finally managed to convince the telemarketer at the other end that she did *not* want to switch her long distance carrier.

The third call came shortly after that. Her mother wanted to hear about Elise's delivery.

Sheryl sank onto the sofa. This conversation would

take a lot longer than the one she'd just had with the telemarketer, she knew. Scratching Button's ears absently, she told her mother what had happened at the hospital…and afterward. The news that Sheryl had failed to perform her coaching duties surprised Joan Hancock. The news of her breakup with Brian left her stuttering.

"But…but…you two were almost engaged!"

"'Almost' is the operative word, Mom."

"I don't understand. What happened?"

Sighing, Sheryl crossed her ankles on the sturdy bleached-oak plank that served as her coffee table. She'd abandoned her now almost buttonless denim dress for a cool, gauzy turquoise top and matching flowered leggings. With Button snuggled against her thighs, she tried to explain to her mother the feelings she'd only recently discovered herself.

"We decided that we wanted more than what we had together."

"You don't even know *what* you had! You'd better think twice, Sheryl Ann Hancock, before you let a man like Brian slip through your fingers."

Joan's voice took on the brittle edge her daughter recognized all too well. Mentally, Sheryl braced herself.

"He's so nice," her mother argued. "So reliable. He'd never leave you to lie awake at night wondering where he was, or make you worry about whether he had a decent meal or remembered to take his blood pressure medicine."

Recalling the near-sleepless night she'd just spent wondering and worrying about Harry, Sheryl could only agree.

"No, he wouldn't."

"Call him," Joan urged. "Brian loves you. I know he does. Tell him you made a mistake. Tell him you want to patch things up. And I suggest you do it before that so-called friend of yours sinks her claws in him."

Sheryl blinked at the acid comment. "What are you talking about?"

"Oh, come on! I may get up to Albuquerque only a few times a month, but that's more than enough for me to see that Elise knows very well what a prize Brian is, if you don't. She's been mooning after him ever since her divorce."

Struck, Sheryl thought back over the past few months. Elise hadn't exactly mooned over Brian, but she, like Joan, was forever singing his praises. Then there was that kiss at the hospital to consider, when Elise had dragged the man down by his tie. And the substitute father's wide-eyed wonder in the baby.

A huge grin tracked across Sheryl's face. Harry had all but wiped away the ache in her heart caused by her breakup with Brian. She and the marshal might or might not ever reach the "almost" point she'd reached with Brian. Right now, though, she couldn't think of anything that would please her more than for her two best friends to find the same passion, the same wild need, that she'd discovered in Harry's arms.

She sprang up, dislodging the sleeping dog in the process. He gave her a disgusted look and plopped down again.

"I've gotta go, Mom. I have to swing by Elise's house to pick up some clothes for her. Then I'm heading for the hospital. She and I need to talk."

"Yes," her mother sniffed. "You do."

Still grinning, Sheryl hung up and headed for the bedroom. She was halfway across the room when the phone rang again. She spun around, ignoring the protest of her bruised heel, and grabbed the phone.

It had to be Harry this time!

"Miss Hancock?"

She swallowed her swift disappointment. "Yes?"

"My name is Don Ortega. I'm an attorney representing a woman you know as Mrs. Inga Gunderson."

"Oh! Yes, I think I heard your name mentioned."

"I understand from Marshal Everett Sloan that you're keeping my client's dog."

She eyed the animal sprawled in blissful abandon on her sofa.

"Well, I'm not sure who's keeping whom, but he's here. Why? Does Mrs. Gunderson want me to take him to someone else?"

She frowned, wondering why the thought of losing her uninvited houseguest didn't fill her with instant elation. The mutt had chewed up her underwear, sprayed her dining-room chair and led her on a not-so-merry chase through the apartment complex this morning. Even worse, his sharp claws had brought Harry jerking straight up this morning, as they had her more than once the past few nights. She ought to be dancing with joy at the prospect of dumping him on some other unsuspecting victim.

Instead, she breathed an inexplicable sigh of relief when the lawyer responded to her question with a negative.

"No, my client doesn't have any close friends or acquaintances in Albuquerque. She's just worried about her, er, Butty-boo. She asked me to check with you and find out if you'd given him his heartworm pill," he finished on a dry note.

"I didn't know he needed one."

"According to my client, he has to have one today. She was quite insistent about it. Evidently, her dog almost died last year when the worms got into his bloodstream and wrapped around his heart."

The gruesome description made Sheryl gulp.

"She says that he could pick up another infestation if he misses even one dose of the medication," Ortega advised her.

"So where can I get this medication?"

"If you wouldn't mind going to the pet store on Menaul, where Mrs. Gunderson does business, you can pick up the pills and charge them to her account. My client has instructed me to call ahead and authorize the expenditure."

"Well…"

She hesitated, wondering if she should contact Harry or Ev Sloan before she acceded to the attorney's request. But Ev had vouched for the lawyer himself, she recalled, swearing that he was tough but straight. Evidently, he also cared enough about his clients to relay their concern for their pets.

"I don't mind," she told Ortega. "Give me the address of this store."

She jotted it down just below the list of items Elise had asked her to bring to the hospital.

"I was just leaving to visit a friend at University Hospital. I'll stop at the pet store on my way."

"Thank you, Miss Hancock. I'm sure my client will be most grateful."

His client, Sheryl discovered when she walked out of the pet store a little over an hour later, was more than grateful. She was lying in wait for her...in the form of two men with slicked-back hair, unsmiling eyes, shiny gray suits and black turtlenecks that must have made them miserable in Albuquerque's sweltering heat.

One of the men appeared at Sheryl's side just as she unlocked her car door. The other materialized from behind a parked car. Before she had done more than glance at them, before she could grasp their intent, before she could scream or even try to twist away, the shorter of the men slapped a folded handkerchief over her mouth.

She fought for two or three seconds. Two or three breaths. Then the street and the car and the gray suits tilted crazily. Another breath, and they disappeared in a haze of blackness.

Chapter 12

"Dammit, where is she?"

Harry paced the task force operations center like a caged, hungry and very irritated panther. He'd been trying to reach Sheryl since just after ten, and it was now almost three.

Ev Sloan leaned back in his chair and watched his partner's restless prowling. Like Harry's, his face showed the effects of his previous long night in the tired lines and gray shadows under his eyes.

"Want me to call central dispatch and have them put out an APB?"

Harry shoved his hands in his pockets and jiggled his loose change. His gut urged him to agree to the all-points bulletin, but this morning's fiasco held him back. He didn't want to use up any more chits with the Albuquerque police than he already had. Sheryl was probably out shopping or visiting friends. A patrol car had already swung by her apartment and verified that her car wasn't in its assigned slot…and the door to her place was shut!

"We'll hold off on the APB," he growled.

"Whatever you say." Ev scraped a hand across the stubble on his chin. "I'm getting too old for this kind of work. I used to get an adrenaline fix from a takedown like last night's that would last me for weeks. Now all I want to do is to nail this bastard Gunderson, go home, kick off my shoes and grab the remote."

"I'll settle for seeing my son's T-ball team bring in just one run," Fay put in with a smile.

The other two men at the conference table took up the refrain. They'd joined the team this morning, each an expert in his own field. While they tossed desultory comments about the best way to ease the strain that gripped them all, Harry paced the length of the room again, his change jingling.

Why the hell couldn't he shake this edgy, unfinished feeling that had been with him almost since he'd left Sheryl this morning?

Because he'd left Sheryl this morning.

He had to face the truth. The way he'd walked out of her arms and her apartment was eating at him from the inside out. It didn't do any good to remind himself that he'd had to get back to the command center and attend to the up-channel reports from the drug bust last night. Or that he'd wanted another go at Inga Gunderson. The blasted woman still refused to talk, except to pester Harry and Ev and her lawyer, Don Ortega, with repeated instructions on the care and feeding of her precious Button. Harry had come out of this morning's session at the detention center so tight jawed with frustration that his back teeth ached.

A flash message from the CIA with the news that they'd traced the six canisters of depleted uranium to Rio de Janeiro had only added to his mounting tension. The shipment had to be heading for the States any day now.

Any hour.

As a result of that message, the task force had redoubled its efforts. Fay had asked the FAA to send out an alert to every airport manager in the four-state area, then contacted her highway patrol counterparts. Ev had pulled in two more deputy marshals from the Albuquerque office. The added personnel were following up every lead, however tenuous, including an unconfirmed report of a visit to the city by two thugs who supposedly strong-armed for a known illegal arms dealer.

Harry had plenty to occupy his mind…yet he'd interrupted his work a half-dozen times in the past five hours to call Sheryl. Between calls, he'd find himself thinking of her at every unguarded moment.

His fists closed around the loose coins. He shouldn't have just walked out like that. After what they'd shared, his refusal to make any promises must have hit her like a slap in the face.

What the hell kind of promises could he make? he thought savagely. That he'd return to her apartment tonight? Tomorrow night? For however long he was in town? That he'd swing through Albuquerque every few months and take her up on the offer that shimmered in her green eyes when he'd left this morning? That he'd ask her to share his life…or at least the few weeks of relatively normal life he enjoyed before he hit the road again?

The thought of sharing any kind of a life with Sheryl grabbed at Harry with a force that sucked the air right out of his lungs. He stared at the wall, the edge of the coins cutting into his palm. For a moment, he let himself contemplate a future that included nights like last night. Mornings like the one he'd woken up to today.

He wouldn't even mind the hairy little mutt digging his claws into his groin again just to hear Sheryl's laughter. His throat closed at the memory of those helpless giggles and the way she'd fallen back on the bed, her hair spilling across the blanket and her rosy-tipped breasts peaking in the cool air-conditioning.

Angrily, he shook his head to clear the erotic image. Why in the world was he putting himself through this? He'd learned the hard way that fugitive operations and a stable home life didn't make for a compatible mix. Sheryl, too, had seen firsthand her parents' inability to sustain a long-distance marriage. Harry had damned well better stop thinking about impossible futures and concentrate on right here, right now.

Which brought him back full circle to the question of where Sheryl was at this moment. More irritable and edgy than ever, he strode back to the conference table and reached for the phone.

"Maybe her friend in the hospital knows where she is," he said curtly in answer to Ev's quizzical look. "I'll make one more call, then we need to go over today's scheduled flights into every major airport in the four-state area. I want copies of all passenger lists and cargo manifests as soon as they're filed."

The operator patched him though to University Hospital, which in turn connected him with Elise Hart's room. Harry recognized instantly the male voice that answered on the second ring. What did Sheryl's former boyfriend do—live at the damned hospital?

Curtly, he identified himself. "This is Harry MacMillan. I'm trying to reach Sheryl."

Just as curtly, Brian Mitchell responded. "She's not here."

"Do you know where she is?"

"No." Mitchell hesitated, then continued in a less abrupt tone. "As a matter of fact, I was thinking of calling you, Marshal. Sheryl told Elise that she'd swing by her house to pick up some clean clothes before she came to the hospital this morning. She hasn't shown up and doesn't answer her phone."

Harry stiffened. The prickly sixth sense that had been nagging at him all day vaulted into full-fledged alarm.

"We're a little worried about her," Brian finished.

A little worried! Christ!

"I'll check it out."

The real-estate-agent's voice sharpened once again. "She's okay, isn't she? This manhunt you pulled her into hasn't put her in danger."

"I'll check it out."

"I want you to notify me immediately when you find her!"

Yeah, right. Harry palmed him off with a half promise and slammed the phone down. Then he snatched his jacket off the back of a chair and headed for the door.

"Call the APD, Ev. Ask them to put out that all-points. And ask them to have their locksmith meet me at Sheryl's apartment."

Ev took one look at his partner's face and grabbed for the phone. "Right away!"

Harry wheeled the souped-up sedan out of the underground parking garage. The tires whined on the hot asphalt. Merging the vehicle into the light weekend traffic flow, he willed himself into a state of rigid control. He'd carried a five-pointed gold star too long to give in to the concern churning like bile in his belly.

Adobe-fronted strip malls and tree-shaded residences whizzed by. Ahead, the Sandia Mountains loomed brownish gray against an endless blue sky. The stutter of a jackhammer cut through the heat of the afternoon.

The sights and sounds registered on Harry's consciousness, but didn't penetrate. His mind was spinning with possibilities. Sheryl could have gone in to work. No one had answered at the Monzano Branch when he'd called earlier, but they might not answer the phones during off-hours.

She could be running errands. The time could have slipped away from her, and she'd forgotten her promise to stop by the hospital this morning.

Or she might have taken off on another jaunt with that damned dog. Hell, she'd chased him barefoot around the whole complex only this morning and left her door open to all comers.

His hands fisted on the steering wheel. He'd strangle her! If she'd ignored all security measures again and scared the hell out of him like this, he'd strangle her...right after he locked the door behind them, tumbled her onto the bed and told her just how much he'd hated leaving her this morning!

Assuming, a small, cold corner of his mind countered, that Sheryl was in any state to hear him.

At that moment, she wasn't.

Her stomach swirled with nausea. Her throat burned. Black spots danced under her closed lids.

In a desperate effort to clear her blurred vision, Sheryl lifted her head an inch or two. Even that slight movement brought an acrid taste into her dry, parched throat and made her senses swim. Moaning, she let her head fall. It hit the bare mattress with a soft plop, raising a musty cloud of dust motes.

"Ya back with us, sweetheart?"

The thin, nasal voice drifted through the sickening haze. Sheryl's clogged mind had barely separated the words enough to make sense of them when a deeper, almost rasping voice came from somewhere above and behind her.

"The next time you do a broad, you idiot, cut the dosage."

"Hey, enough already! You been on my back for hours about that."

"Yeah?"

The vicious snarl scraped across Sheryl's skin like a dull knife. "Who do you think is gonna be on our backs if we miss this drop?"

"She's coming 'round, ain't she?"

"It's about damn time."

Without warning, a palm cracked against Sheryl's cheek.

"Come on, wake up."

Gasping at the pain that splintered across her face, she fought to bring the figure bending over her into focus. A greasy shine appeared...black hair, slicked back, reflecting the light of the single overhead bulb.

She blinked. Her lids gritted like sandpaper against her eyes. Slowly, she made out a wide, unshaven jaw above a black turtleneck. A pair of unsmiling eyes in a face some people might have considered handsome.

"We ain't gonna hurt you."

"You..." She swiped her tongue around her cottony mouth. "You...just...did."

"That little love tap?" The stranger snorted and dug a hand into her armpit. "Come on, sit up and take a drink. We gotta talk."

The mists fogging Sheryl's mind shredded enough for her to grasp the fact her wrists were tied behind her. Fear spurted like ice water through her veins. Her feet dropped to the floor with a thump, first one, then the other. She swayed, dizzy and confused and more scared than she'd ever been before. The grip on her arm held her upright.

Another figure appeared from the dimness to her side, holding a glass. When he shoved it at her lips,

Sheryl shrank away. A fist buried itself in her hair, yanked her head back.

"It's just water. Drink it."

With the glass chinking against her teeth, she didn't have a whole lot of choice. Most of the tepid liquid ran down her chin, but enough got through her teeth to satisfy the pourer.

The fist loosened. Sheryl brought her head up and eased the ache in her neck. Gradually, the black swirls in front of her eyes subsided

"Wh…? Where am I?"

The words came out in a croak, but Slick Hair understood them. He flicked an impatient hand.

"It don't matter where you are. What matters is where you're going."

She swallowed painfully. Her heart thumping with fear, she met her kidnapper's unsmiling gaze.

"Where am I going?"

A snigger sounded beside her. "That's what you're gonna tell us, sweetheart."

She swung her head toward the second man. Like Slick Hair, this one also wore a black turtleneck and a shiny gray suit. It must be some kind of uniform, she thought with a touch of hysteria. He had small, pinched eyes and a nasal pitch that grated on her ears. He came from somewhere east of New Mexico, obviously. Or maybe he owed that whine to the fact that someone or something had flattened his nose against his face.

Slick Hair scraped a chair across the bare wood floor, twisted it around and straddled the seat. With Broken Nose hovering at his shoulder, he smiled thinly.

"We need to have us a little chat, Sheryl." At her start of surprise, his smile took on a sadistic edge. "What? You don't think we know your name? Of course we know it. We got it from Inga this morning."

Despite her fear and the pain lancing through her face and wrists, her head had cleared enough by now for her to grasp that the men confronting her had some connection to Harry's investigation. She just hadn't expected them to admit it so readily.

"How…?" She swallowed. "How did you talk to Inga? She's in…"

"In jail?" Slick Hair waved a hand, dismissing the small irritation of police custody. "Those bastards at the detention center wouldn't allow her more than her one damn call to her lawyer, but Inga's a shrewd old broad. She got this Ortega guy to call the shop and let our little friend there know you were coming."

"The pet shop?"

"Yeah," Broken Nose put in. "We been hangin' out there, waiting for Inga to show. We was worried when we heard the cops snatched her, but like Big Ja—" He caught himself. "Like my friend here says, she's a smart old broad. We just waited, and sure enough, she sent you."

Slick Hair folded his forearms across the back of the chair. His eyes settled on her face.

"So, you wanna tell us about the postcard?"

She tried to bluff it out. "What postcard?"

"The one that come in from Rio, Sheryl. The one from Rio."

"I don't know what you're talking about. No one sent me any postcards, from Rio or anywhere else."

"Come on, sweetheart," Broken Nose whined. "We got contacts, ya know. It didn't take no undercover dick to find out you work at a post office. Since Inga sent you to the shop, you gotta have the information we want."

"No, I—"

In a move so swift that Sheryl didn't even see it coming, Slick Hair's arm whipped out. The back-handed blow sent her tumbling sideways onto the bare mattress. She lay there for endless seconds, biting her lip against the pinwheeling pain. She wouldn't cry! She wouldn't give in to the fear coursing through her!

Harry was looking for these men or their partner in crime. He'd soon come looking for her, too. She didn't know how long she'd been out, or where she was now, or what was going to happen next, but she just had to hold on. Find out what she could. Get word to Harry somehow.

Slowly, awkwardly, she pushed herself up on one elbow and faced her captors.

"Now, tell us about the card from Rio, Sheryl."

"Wh…?" She wet her lips. "What do you want to know?"

Slick Hair smiled again, his thin lips slicing across the strong planes of his face. "Smart girl. Just tell me what Paul wrote on the back."

Bitterly regretting that she'd ever peeked at Inga Gunderson's mail, much less harbored any concern for her welfare, Sheryl summoned a mental picture of the bright, gaudy Carnival street scene. The words on the back of the card formed, went hazy, reformed.

"'Hi to my favorite aunt,'" she recited dully. "'I've

been dancing in the streets for the past five days. Wish you were here.'"

"Five days!"

Broken Nose did a quick turn about the room. It was empty of all but a rickety table, the two chairs and the cot she sat on, Sheryl saw. A blanket covered the only window.

"Five days past the date of the last drop," the smaller man continued excitedly. "Lessee. Last time, we picked up the stuff on the third. Five days past that would make it the eighth. Tomorrow. Damn! We got another whole day to wait."

Slick Hair didn't move, didn't take his eyes off Sheryl's face. With everything in her, she tried not to flinch as he reached out and twisted a hand through her hair.

"I don't think you're giving it to us straight," he said softly, bringing her face to within inches of his own. "You sure that postcard said 'five' days, Sheryl? Think hard. Real hard."

"Yes," she gasped. "Yes, I'm sure."

Slick Hair looked into her eyes for another few moments. "Get the needle," he told his partner quietly.

She tried to jerk away. "No!"

His painful grip kept her still.

"It's just a little drug we got from a friendly doc, Sheryl. It'll help you remember. Help you get the details right."

There was no way she was going to allow these men to stick a needle in her. God only knows who had used it before or what drug they'd pump into her.

"Maybe… Maybe it said 'four days.'"

Satisfaction flared in the eyes so close to her own. "Maybe it did, Sheryl."

"Jesus!" Broken Nose thumped his fist against his shiny pantleg. "That's tonight!"

"So it is," Slick Hair mused. "That must be why Inga sent you to us, Sheryl. She was probably in a real sweat, knowin' Paul was coming in tonight and no one would be there to greet him. Well, we'll be there."

Sheryl closed her eyes in an agony of remorse. Harry! I'm sorry! I'm so sorry.

"You'll be there, too," Slick Hair finished, easing his grip on her hair. "If Paul doesn't show, we're gonna be real, real unhappy with you."

The threat should have paralyzed her with fear. Instead, it slowly penetrated her despair and lit a tiny spark of anger. She hoped Paul Gunderson *did* show. She hoped he walked off a plane tonight and found not only these creeps, but a small army of law enforcement officials waiting for him. She hoped to hell she was there to see it when Harry took Gunderson and these two goons down.

Which he would! She knew he would! These men didn't realize that Harry would tear the city apart when he discovered she was missing. He'd find her car, trace her to the pet store. It wouldn't take him long to tie that visit back to Inga Gunderson. Maybe he already had.

He'd find a way to make Inga talk.

He had to!

Chapter 13

Ev Sloan waited for Harry on the steps of the Bernalilo County Detention Center. Even though the sun had dropped behind the cluster of downtown buildings and shadows stretched across the street, sweat streaked Ev's face and plastered his shirt to his chest. As he'd told Fay just before he'd left her at the operations center, he sincerely hoped he'd never have to go through again what he'd experienced since the Albuquerque police had located Sheryl Hancock's abandoned car three hellish hours ago.

His gut had twisted at the realization that the woman he'd worked with for the past couple of days had been snatched right off the street. As deep as it went, his worry over Sheryl's status didn't begin to compare with Harry's. Not that MacMillan's wrenching desperation showed to anyone who didn't know him. Ev had worked with him long enough to recognize the signs, though. The stark fury, quickly masked. The fear, even more quickly hidden. The cold, implacable determination that had driven him every minute since they'd found the car.

Thank God for the crumpled piece of paper under the Camry's front seat. Sheryl's hand-scribbled list had led them to the pet shop and to the nervous shop owner, who'd IDed the two men who'd followed their victim out of the store. The process of identifying them might have taken a whole lot longer than it had if Harry hadn't instantly connected them to the two strong-arms rumored to have been sighted in Albuquerque. With the FBI's help, they now had names, backgrounds and mug shots of both men. Through a screening of Sheryl's phone calls this morning, they also had a link to Don Ortega.

Attorney and client were waiting inside for them now. Ev didn't kid himself. This interview was going to be a rough one. He'd known that since Harry had stalked out of the task force command center a half hour ago, instructing Ev to meet him at the detention center. But he didn't realize how rough until he saw MacMillan climbing out of the sedan that squealed to a stop in front of the steps.

Ev's eyes bugged at the bundle of black-and-white fur wedged under his partner's arm. "Why did you bring that thing down here?"

The car door slammed. "Everyone's got a weak spot in their defenses. Butty-boo here is Inga's."

Spinning around, Ev followed Harry up the steps. "Christ, MacMillan, you're not going to do something stupid like strangle the mutt in front of the old woman to get her to talk?"

"That's one possibility."

"You can't! You know you can't! Ortega will have the DA, the IG, the SPCA and everyone else he can contact down on our heads!"

"Ortega's going to have his hands full dodging a charge of accessory to a kidnapping," Harry shot back.

He shoved through the glass doors, leaving Ev to trail him into the cavernous lobby. The dog tucked under his arm looked around, black eyes bright with interest. He must have spotted something that he didn't like across the lobby because he promptly let loose with a series of shrill yips that ricocheted off the marble walls and hit Ev's eardrums like sharp, piercing arrows.

"Think, man!" he urged over the noise. "Think! You can't hurt the animal, as much as we'd both like to. You can't even threaten to hurt it. You'll jeopardize our case against both Inga and Paul Gunderson if we ever get them to court. They'll say Inga confessed under duress. That she—"

Harry swung around, his eyes blazing. "Right now, our case takes second place to Sheryl Hancock's safety."

His barely contained fury cut Button off in midbark The sudden silence pounded at all three participants in the small drama.

"I dragged her into this," Harry said savagely. "I'm damned well going to get her out."

"By strangling the mutt?"

He blew out a long breath. Some of the fury left his face, but none of the determination. His gaze dropped to the dog. Someone had drawn its facial hair up and tied it with a pink bow. Sheryl, Ev supposed. MacMillan looked about as ridiculous as a man could with the prissy thing tucked under his arm.

"I won't hurt him. I couldn't. If I did, Sheryl would be on my case worse than the old woman. Beats me what either of them sees in the little rat."

Despite his professed dislike for the creature, he knuckled the furry forehead with a gentleness that made Ev blink.

"Then why did you bring him here?"

Harry's hand stilled. When he looked up, his eyes were flat and hard once again.

"If nothing else, I'm going to make damned sure Inga Gunderson knows what happens to animals left unclaimed at the pound for more than three days."

They were heading south on I-25.

That much Sheryl could see from the back floor of the panel truck. Every so often an overhead highway sign would flash in the front windshield where her two captors sat. She'd catch just enough of it to make out a few letters and words.

She shifted on the hard floor, trying to ease the burning ache in her shoulder sockets. The movement only sharpened the pain shooting from her shoulders to her fingertips. She'd long ago given up her futile attempts to twist free of the tape that bound her wrists together behind her back.

All in all, she was more miserable and frightened than she'd ever been in her life. She hadn't drunk anything except the water Slick Hair had poured down her throat hours ago. Hadn't eaten anything since the poppy-seed muffin she'd gulped down before heading out the door this morning. She needed to go to the bathroom, badly, but she'd swallow nails before she asked her kidnappers to stop the truck, escort her to a bathroom and pull down her flowered leggings!

Not that she could ask them even if she wanted to. The bastards had slapped a wide strip of duct tape over her mouth before hauling her outside and hustling her into the waiting truck.

Her physical discomfort sapped her strength. The constant battle to hang on to to her desperate belief that Harry would find her drained it even more.

How long had it been now? Nine hours since she'd walked out of the pet shop on Menaul Avenue? Ten?

How long since Harry had realized that she was missing?

Bright highway lights flashed by in the windshield. Sheryl tried to concentrate on them, tried to keep her mind focused on the tiny details that might help if she had to reconstruct events for Harry after this was all over.

Despite her fierce concentration, doubts and sneaking, sinking fear ate away at her. What if Harry hadn't called her, as he'd promised he would? What if he'd gotten so caught up in his investigation that he didn't have time? Oh, God, what if he didn't even know she was missing?

She closed her eyes, fighting the panic that threatened to swamp her.

He said he'd call. He'd promised he would. What Harry promised, he'd do. She'd learned that much about him in the short, intense time they'd been together. He'd called her sometime today. She knew he had. And when she hadn't answered, he'd started looking.

He'd find her.

Battling fiercely with her incipient panic, she almost missed the click of directional signals. A moment later, the truck slowed and banked into a turn. Signs flashed by overhead, but Sheryl couldn't catch the lettering.

After another mile or so, Broken Nose twisted around. "It's show time, doll. You'd better hope our star performer shows."

Dragging a folded moving pad from under his seat, he shook it out and tossed it over her. Total blackness surrounded her, along with the stink of mildew and motor oil. Sheryl closed her eyes and prayed that she'd see Harry when she opened them.

She didn't.

When the pad was jerked away, Broken Nose loomed over her once more. His face was a grotesque mask of shadows in the diffused light of the truck's interior.

"Come on, sweetheart," he whined. "You're gonna wait inside. We don't want no nosy Customs inspectors catchin' sight of you in the truck, do we?"

Wrapping his paw around her elbow, he hauled her out of the truck. Pain zigzagged like white, agonizing lightning up and down Sheryl's arm. She couldn't breathe, let alone groan, through the duct tape sealing her mouth.

Broken Nose hauled her to her feet outside the truck

and hustled her toward one of the rear doors in a corrugated steel hangar. Sheryl stumbled along beside him, trying desperately to clear her head of the pain and get her bearings. The air she dragged in through her nostrils carried with it the unmistakable bite of jet fuel fumes. The distant whine of engines revving up confirmed she was at the airport.

The moment her captor shoved her inside the huge, steel-sided building, she recognized the cavernous, shadowy interior. She could never forget it! She'd worked at rotation at the airport cargo-handling facility as a young rookie, years ago, and had counted the months until she'd gained enough seniority to qualify for another opening. Palletizing the sacks of mail that came into this building from the central processing center downtown for air shipment was backbreaking, dirty work.

Sure enough, she spotted a long row of web-covered pallets in the postal service's caged-off portion of the hangar. Desperately, she searched the dimly lit area for someone she might know, someone who might see her. Before she could locate any movement in the vast, echoing facility, Broken Nose shouldered open a door and pushed her into what looked like a heating/air-conditioning room. In the weak moonlight filtering through the single, dust-streaked window, Sheryl saw a litter of discarded web cargo straps, empty crates and broken chairs amid the rusted duct pipes.

Her captor surveyed the dust-covered floor and grunted in satisfaction. "Ain't nobody been in since I scouted this place out two days ago."

Roughly, he dragged Sheryl across the room and shoved her down onto a tangle of web cargo straps. She landed awkwardly on one knee. A hard hand in her back sent her tumbling onto her hip. Her elbow hit the concrete floor beneath the straps. Searing pain jolted into her shoulder, blinding her. Tears filled her eyes. She barely heard the snap as Broken Nose pulled another length of tape from his roll, barely felt her ankles jammed against a pipe and lashed together.

She felt the fist that buried itself in her hair, though, and a painful jerk as he brought her face around to his.

"We're gonna be right outside, see? Pickin' up our cargo soon's the lamebrain from Customs clears it. Everything goes okay, I'll come back for you."

His fist tightened in her hair.

"Anything goes wrong, I might or might not come back for you. If I don't, maybe someone'll find you in a week or a month. Or maybe they won't. You won't be so pretty when they do."

Grinning maliciously, he stroked a finger down her cheek. Sheryl couldn't move enough to flinch from his touch, but she put every drop of loathing she could into the look she sent him. Laughing, he left her in the musty darkness.

She lay, half on her side, half on her back, breathing in dust motes and the acrid scent of her own fear. Her relief that they'd left her for even a few moments was almost as great as her discomfort. Her shoulder was on fire. Her elbow throbbed. The metal clasp on one of the web straps gouged into her hip.

She didn't care. For the first time since she'd walked

out of the pet store this morning, she was out of her captor's sight. Ignoring her various aches and pains, she twisted and turned, pulling at the tape binding her ankles to the pipe. The metal pole didn't budge, nor did the tape give, but she did manage to generate a small shower of rust particles and bugs. Praying that none of the insects that dropped down on her were of the biting variety, she tugged and twisted and pushed and pulled.

By the time she conceded defeat, she was filmed with sweat and rust and wheezing in air through her nose. For a moment, the panic she'd kept at bay for so many hours almost swamped her.

Where was Harry? Why hadn't he tracked her down? He was a U.S. marshal, for God's sake? He was supposed to be able to find anyone. Where was he?

Gradually, she fought down her panic. Slowly, she got her breath back. Blinking the sweat from her eyes, she shifted on the pile of straps to try again. Another pain shot up from her elbow. The edge of a strap buckle dug into her hip.

Suddenly, Sheryl froze. The strap buckles! The metal tongue of the clasp that connected the web straps had sharp edges. She'd cut herself on the damned things often enough as a rookie. If she could get a grip on one of the buckles, get the clasp open…

Sweating, straining, wiggling as much as her ankles would allow, Sheryl groped the pile underneath her. Her slick fingers found a metal apparatus, pulled open the hasp. It slipped away from her and closed with a snap. She grabbed the buckle again, holding it awkwardly with one hand.

Grimly determined now, she fumbled one of the thick straps into her hand. If she could just pry the buckle open enough...

Yes!

Too excited for caution, she slid a fingertip along the edge of the hasp. Instantly, warm blood welled from the slicing cut.

The thing was as sharp as she remembered!

Her heart thumping, she went to work on the duct tape. She'd freed her wrists and was working on her ankles when a sharp rap shattered the glass in the dusty window. Pieces fell to the concrete. The small tinkles reverberated like shots in Sheryl's head.

An arm reached inside and fumbled for the lock.

With a burst of strength, Sheryl pulled apart the remaining half inch of duct tape. She scrambled to her feet, still gripping the metal clasp. It wasn't much of a weapon, but it was all she had.

Slowly, the window screeched upward. A moment later, a figure covered in black from head to toe climbed through. Even before he holstered his weapon and whipped off his ski mask, Sheryl had recognized the lean, muscular body.

"Harry!"

She threw herself across the room, broken glass crunching like popcorn under her feet. He crushed her against his chest.

"Are you all right?" he asked, his voice urgent in her ear.

She dismissed burning shoulders and aching wrists and cut fingers. "Yes."

"Thank God!"

His fierce embrace squeezed the air from Sheryl's lungs. She didn't care. At this moment, breathing didn't concern her. All that mattered was the feel of Harry's arms around her. Which didn't explain why she promptly burst into tears.

"It's all right, sweetheart," he soothed, his voice low and ragged. "It's all right. I'm here."

She leaned back, swallowing desperately, and stared up at him through a sheen of tears. "What took you so darned long?"

"It took me a while to convince Inga to talk."

"How…?" She gulped. "How did you do that?"

A small, tight smile flitted across Harry's face. "I got a little help from Button."

"From Button!"

He hustled her toward the window. "I'll tell you about it later. Right now, I just want to get you out of here. Then I'm going after the bastards who kidnapped you. My whole team's outside, ready to move in as soon as you're clear."

"No!" Sheryl spun around and grabbed at him with both hands. "You can't take those two down. Not yet! They're waiting for Paul Gunderson. He's coming in tonight, Harry. Tonight!"

"I know."

His slow, satisfied reply sent a shiver down her back. For a moment Sheryl almost didn't recognize the man who stared at her. His face could have been cut from rock.

Almost as quickly as it appeared, the fierceness left

his eyes. In its place came a look that made her blink through the blur of her tears.

"Come on, sweetheart. Let's get you out of here."

Her fingers dug into the sleeves of his black windbreaker. She had to tell him. Had to let him know before he shoved her through the window and turned back into danger.

"Harry, I love you. I...I know it's too soon for commitments and promises and almost-anythings between us, but I—"

He cut off her disjointed declaration with a swift, hard, soul-shattering kiss.

"I love you, too. I suspected it this morning, when all I could think about was getting back to you. I knew it this afternoon, when we found your car." His jaw worked. "I don't *ever* want to go through that again, so let's get you the hell out of here. Now!"

They almost made it.

Her heart singing, Sheryl started for the window once more. Broken glass crunched under her feet and almost covered the sound of the door opening behind them.

"What the hell...?"

Harry spun around, yanking her behind him. Off balance and flailing for a hold, Sheryl didn't see him reach for his gun. Broken Nose did, though.

"Don't do it!" he shouted. Desperation added an octave to his high-pitched whine. "Your hand moves another inch and I swear to God, I'll put one of these hot slugs through you and the bitch both!"

Harry froze. A single glance at the oversized barrel

on the weapon in the man's hand confirmed that it was engineered to fire uranium-tipped cop-killer bullets. The same kind of bullets that had ripped right through his best friend's body armor. Harry was willing to stop a bullet to protect Sheryl, but he couldn't, wouldn't, take the chance that it might plow right through him and into her, as well.

His pulse hammering, he lifted both hands clear of his sides. His Smith & Wesson sat like a dead weight in its holster just under his armpit.

"Yeah, yeah! That's better."

Even in the dim moonglow, Harry recognized the man whose flattened nose and jet-black hair he'd memorized from a mug shot less than an hour ago.

"All right, D'Agustino. Don't get crazy here and maybe we can work a deal."

"Jesus! You know who I am?"

"You and your partner both. You might as well give it up now. We've got this place surrounded."

"I knew it! I knew them guys in the coveralls weren't no wrench benders, not with them bulges under their arms. That's why I come running back for the broad. She's my ticket outta here."

Harry felt Sheryl go rigid against his back. Her fingers gripped his shirt. The image of her pinned helplessly against this killer raised a red haze in front of his eyes. Coldly, he blinked it away.

"She's not going anywhere with you, D'Agustino."

"Oh, yeah! Guess again."

The snick of a hammer cocking back added emphasis to the sneering reply.

Harry started to speak, and almost strangled on an indrawn breath. His whole body stiffened at the feel of a hand sliding around his rib cage. Without seeming to move, he brought his arms in just enough to cover Sheryl's reach for his holstered weapon.

Sweat rolled down his temples as her fingers slid under his arm. Sheryl hated guns! They made her nervous. She'd told him so more than once. She probably didn't have the faintest idea how to use one!

At that moment, Harry figured he had two options. He could throw himself at D'Agustino and hope to beat a bullet to the punch, or he could trust the woman behind him to figure out which end of a .357 was which.

It didn't even come close to a choice. He'd take his chances with Sheryl over this punk any day.

"Think about it D'Agustino," he said, trying desperately to buy her some time. "We know who you are. We know you've been working with Paul Gunderson. I have two dozen men waiting to greet him when his plane touches down a few minutes from now."

"Yeah, well, me and Sheryl ain't waiting around for that. Get over here, bitch!"

Harry could smell the man's fear. Hear it in his high, grating whine.

"You might get away this time, but we'll come after you. All of us. The FBI. The U.S. Marshals Service. Customs. Better give yourself up now. Talk to us."

"Don't you understand! I'm a dead man if Big Jake hears I cut a deal with the feds!"

"You're a dead man if you don't."

"No! No, I ain't!"

He knew the instant D'Agustino's gun came up that time had just run out.

He dived across the room.

A shot exploded an inch from his ear.

Sheryl didn't kill the little bastard. She didn't even wound him. But she startled him just enough to throw off his aim.

His gun barrel spit red flame. A finger of fire seared across Harry's cheek. The wild shot ricocheted off a pipe and gouged into the ceiling at precisely the same instant his fist smashed into an already flattened nose with a satisfying, bone-crunching force.

D'Agustino reared back, howling. A bruising left fist followed the right. The man crumpled like a sack of stones.

His chest heaving, Harry reached down and jerked the specially crafted .45 out of his hand. Although the thug showed no signs of moving any time soon, he kept the gun trained at his heart. Over the prone body, his anxious gaze found Sheryl.

"You okay?"

She nodded, her face paper white in the dimness. Then, incredibly, she produced a shaky, strained smile.

"You'd better cuff him or…or do whatever it is you marshals do. We've got a plane to meet."

Chapter 14

"I'm not leaving."

Sheryl folded arms encased in the too-long sleeves of a black windbreaker and glared at Deputy Marshal Ev Sloan. He fired back with an equally stubborn look.

"It could get nasty around here. Nasti*er*," he amended with a glance at the two men huddled back to back on the asphalt a few yards away, their hands cuffed behind their backs. Fay and another officer stood over them, reading them their rights.

"I want to stay," Sheryl insisted. "I need to see this."

"This isn't any place for civilians. We don't have time to—"

"It's okay, Ev."

Harry nodded his thanks to the medic who'd just taped a gauze bandage on his upper cheek. He crossed the asphalt to the task force command vehicle, his gaze on the woman hunched in the front seat.

"She's part of the team."

His quiet words dissolved the last of Sheryl's own secret doubts. She couldn't quite believe that she was sitting in a truck that bristled with more antennas than a porcupine on a bad-quill day, watching while an army of law enforcement agencies checked their weapons and coordinated last-minute details for the takedown of a smuggler and suspected killer. Or that she'd pulled out a .357 Magnum and squeezed a trigger herself mere moments ago. Until Harry MacMillan had charged into her life, she'd only experienced this kind of Ramboesque excitement through movies and TV.

This wasn't a movie, though. She had the bruises and the bunched-up knot of fear in her stomach to prove it. This was real. This was life or death, and Harry was right in the middle of it. There was no way Sheryl was going to leave, as Ev insisted, while Harry calmly walked right back into the line of fire.

Besides, she and Harry had a conversation to finish. They'd tossed around a few words such as "love" and "commitment" and "promises" in that dark, dirty storeroom. Sheryl wanted more than words.

She wouldn't get them any time soon, she saw. Having assured himself she'd sustained no serious injury, and having had the powder burn on his cheek attended to, the marshal was ready for action. More than ready. In the glow from the command vehicle's overhead light, his whiskey-gold eyes gleamed with barely restrained impatience. He paused before her, holding himself in check long enough to brush a knuckle down her cheek.

"I don't want to worry about you any more than I already have today. Promise me that you'll stay in the command vehicle."

"I promise."

"Ev told you that we have a U.S. Marshals Service plane standing by. If Paul Gunderson's aboard the incoming aircraft and we take him down…"

"You will!" Sheryl said fiercely. "I know you will!"

His knuckle stilled. The glint in his eyes turned feral. "Yes, I will."

She bit down her lower lip, waiting for him to come back to her. A moment later, the back of his hand resumed its slow stroke.

"I might not get a chance to talk to you after the bust. I'll have to bundle Gunderson aboard our plane and get him and his two pals back to Washington for arraignment."

"I know."

Cupping her chin, he turned her face a few more degrees into the light. He stared down at her, as if imprinting her features on his memory.

Sheryl could have wished for a better image for him to take with him. Her cheeks still carried traces of the rust and squashed bugs that had rained down on her from the overhead pipes during her desperate escape attempt. Her hair frizzed all over her head. If she'd had on a lick of makeup when she'd left her apartment so many hours ago, she'd long since chewed or rubbed or cried it off.

Harry didn't seem to mind the bugs or frizz or total lack of color on her face. His thumb traced a slow path across her lower lip.

"I'll be back. I promise."

Turning her head, Sheryl pressed a kiss to his palm. Her smile was a little ragged around the edges, but she got it into place.

"I'll be waiting."

His hand dropped. A moment later, he disappeared, one of many shadows that melted into the darkness.

Even Ev Sloan deserted Sheryl, vowing that he wasn't going to miss out on the action again. Another deputy marshal took his place in the command vehicle. He introduced himself with a nod, then gave the bank of radios mounted under the dash his total concentration.

Sheryl huddled in her borrowed windbreaker. For some foolish reason, she'd believed that she could never again experience the sick terror that had gripped her those awful hours with Broken Nose and Slick Hair. Now she realized that listening helplessly while the man she loved put his life on the line bred its own brand of terror.

Her heart in her throat, she followed every play in Harry's deadly game.

The game ended less than half an hour later.

To Sheryl's immense relief, the man subsequently identified as Richard Johnson-Paul Gunderson stepped off the cargo plane, tossed up an arm to shield his eyes from a blinding flood of light and promptly threw himself face down on the concrete parking apron.

As a jubilant Ev related to Sheryl, the bastard was brave enough with his mob connections backing him up. Without them, he wet his pants at the first warning shout.

Literally.

"Harry had to scrounge up a clean pair of jeans before he could hustle the bastard aboard our plane," Ev reported gleefully. "The government will probably have to foot the bill for them, but what the hell! We got him, Sher! We got him!"

Grinning from ear to ear, he unbuckled his body armor and tossed it into his gear bag. His webbed belt with its assortment of canisters and ammo clips followed.

"I would've left him to stew in his own juice, so to speak, but then I didn't have to handcuff myself to the man and sit next to him in a small aircraft for the next five or six hours the way Harry did."

"I can see how that would make a difference," Sheryl concurred, her eyes on the twin-engine jet revving up at the end of the runway.

Ev's gear bag hit the back of the command vehicle with a thunk.

"Harry told me to take you home. Fay has to hang around until the Nuclear Regulatory folks finish decertifying the canisters. I told her I'd come back to help with the disposition. You ready to go?"

The small plane with U.S. Marshals Service markings roared down the runway. Sheryl followed its blinking red and white lights until they disappeared into a bank of black clouds.

"I'm ready."

Ev traded places with the marshal who'd manned the command vehicle. He twisted the key in the ignition, then shoved the truck into gear.

"We have to swing by the federal building to pick up the mutt."

"Button?"

Ev's teeth showed white in the airport exit lights. "Harry left him with the security guards when we came chasing out here. As obnoxious as that mutt is, I wouldn't be surprised if one of the guards hasn't skinned him by now and nailed his hide over the front door."

They soon discovered that Button was still in one piece, although the same couldn't be said for the security guards. One sported a long tear in his uniform sleeve. The other pointed out the neat pattern of teeth marks in his leather brogans.

Sheryl apologized profusely and retrieved the indignant animal from the lidded trash can where the guards had stashed him. Button huffed and snuffled and ruffled up his fur, but let himself be carried from the federal building with only a few parting snarls at the guards. After a few greeting snarls at Ev, he settled down on Sheryl's chest.

She buried her nose in his soft, silky fur. The lights of Old Town, only a few blocks from the federal building, sped by unnoticed. The bright wash of stars overhead didn't draw her eyes. Even Ev's excited recounting of the night's tumultuous events barely penetrated. In her mind, she followed the flight of a small silver jet over the Sandias and across New Mexico's wide, flat plains.

He'd be back. He'd promised.

But when?

"Looks like it's going to be next week before Gunderson's arraignment."

Turning her back on the noise of the lively group who'd just arrived at her apartment to celebrate young Master Brian Hart's christening, Sheryl strained to hear Harry's recorded message.

"You have my office number. They can reach me anytime, night or day, if you have an emergency. I'll talk to you soon."

The recorder clicked off.

Frustrated, she hit the repeat button. Except for one short call soon after Harry had arrived in D.C., he and Sheryl had been playing telephone tag for almost three days now. From what she'd gleaned through his brief messages, the man she now thought of as Richard Johnson had held out longer than anyone had expected before finally breaking his stubborn silence. Once the dam gave, the assistant DA working the case had kept Harry busy helping with the briefs for the grand jury. Now, it appeared, he'd have to stay in D.C. until next week's arraignment.

"Sheryl, where are the pretzels? I can't— Oh, I'm sorry, honey. I didn't know you were on the phone."

Replacing the receiver, Sheryl pasted on a smile and turned to face her mother. "I'm not. I was just checking my messages."

"Well? Did he call?"

"Yes, he called."

"Where is he?"

"Still in Washington."

"I want to meet this man. When is he coming back to Albuquerque?"

"He doesn't know."

Her mother's thin, still-attractive face took on the pinched look that Sheryl had seen all too often in her youth. Joan Hancock wanted to say more. That much was obvious from the way she bit down on her lower lip.

Thankfully, she refrained.

She had driven up to Albuquerque from Las Cruces three days ago, after Elise's frantic call informing her that her daughter was missing. She'd stayed through the rest of the weekend, demanding to know every detail about Sheryl's involvement in a search for a dangerous fugitive.

Needless to say, the cautious bits her daughter let drop about the deputy marshal who'd swept in and out of her life hadn't pleased Joan any more than observing Brian Mitchell's growing attachment to his namesake…and his namesake's mother.

The christening ceremony tonight had only added to her disgruntlement. Sheryl and Brian had stood as godparents to the baby. Seeing them together at the altar had rekindled Joan Hancock's grievances against Elise. She was still convinced that the new mother had schemed to steal Sheryl's boyfriend right out from under her nose.

"Just look at her," she griped, pressing the pretzel bowl against the front of the pale-gray silk dress she'd worn to the church. "The way she's making those goo-

goo eyes at Brian, you'd think he'd fathered her child instead of her shiftless ex-husband."

Sheryl's gaze settled on the scene in the living room. Elise had anchored the baby's carrier in a corner of the sofa, where it couldn't be jostled by her two lively boys. They were showing off their baby brother to the assembled crowd with patented propriety. Brian leaned against the arm of the sofa, one finger unconsciously stroking the baby's feathery red curls while he chatted with Elise. Even Button had gotten into the act. Perched on the back of the sofa, he waved his silky tail back and forth and guarded the baby with the regal hauteur that had made the shih tzu so prized by the emperors of China.

It was a picture-perfect family tableau. With all her heart, Sheryl wished everyone in the picture happiness.

She'd told Elise so when the two friends had snatched a half hour alone yesterday. Even now, she had to smile at the emotions that had chased across Elise's face, one after another, like tumbleweeds blown by a high wind. Pain for Sheryl over her break with Brian. Guilty relief that he was free. Disbelief that her friend had fallen for Harry so hard, so fast. Worry that she was in for some hurting times ahead.

Like Joan, Elise couldn't quite believe that her friend had opted to settle for a life of loneliness, broken by days or weeks or even months of companionship. Sheryl couldn't quite believe it, either, but sometime in the past few days, she had.

Joan gave a long, wistful sigh. "Are you sure you and Brian can't patch things up?"

"I'm sure."

Her gaze left the group on the sofa and settled on her daughter's face. "Oh, Sherrie, I hoped you'd do better than I did."

Sheryl's smile softened. "You did fine, Mom."

A haze of tears silvered Joan's green eyes, so like her daughter's. "I wanted you to find someone steady and reliable. Someone who'd be there when you needed him to kiss away your hurts and share your laughter and fix the leaky faucets."

"You taught me to be pretty handy with a wrench," Sheryl replied gently. "And Harry was there when I needed him."

He'd been there, and he'd done more than kiss away her hurts, she acknowledged silently. After her breakup with Brian, he'd driven the hurt right out of her mind. At the airport, he'd wiped away a good measure of her terror and trauma by the simple act of acknowledging her as part of his team.

Along the way, Sheryl thought with an inner smile, he'd also taken her to dizzying heights of pleasure that she'd never dreamed of, let alone experienced. She craved the feel of his hands on her breasts, ached for the brush of his prickly mustache against her skin. She longed to curl up with him on the couch and share a pepperoni-and-pineapple pizza, and watch his face when he bit into one of New Mexico's man-sized peppers.

In short, she wanted whatever moments they could snatch and memories they could make together. Everyone else might count their time together in hours, but Sheryl measured it by the clinging, stubborn love that had taken root in her heart and refused to let go.

Her mother sighed again. "You're going to wait for this man, aren't you? Night after night, week after week?"

"Yes, I am."

Joan lifted a hand and rested a palm against her daughter's cheek. "You're stronger than I was, Sherrie. You'll…you'll make it work."

She hoped so. She sincerely hoped so.

"Come on, Mom. Let's get back to the party."

Despite her conviction that Harry was worth waiting for, Sheryl found the wait more difficult than she'd let on to her mother. The hours seemed to stretch endlessly. Thankfully, she had her job to keep her busy during the day and Button to share her nights.

According to Ev Sloan, she could expect to have the mutt's company for some time to come. He called with the news the evening after little Brian's christening. Just home from work and about to step into the shower, Sheryl ran out of the bathroom and snatched the phone up on the second ring. With some effort, she kept the fierce disappointment from her voice.

"Hi, Ev."

Clutching the towel she'd thrown around her with one hand, she listened to his gleeful news. Patrice Jörgenson/Johnson, aka Inga Gunderson, cut a deal with the federal authorities. In exchange for information about her nephew's activities, she would plead guilty to a lesser battery of charges that would give her the possibility of parole in a few years.

"We're transporting her to D.C. Got a plane standing by. She wants to say goodbye to the mutt first."

"You mean, like, now? Over the phone?"

"Yeah."

The note of disgust in Ev's voice told Sheryl he hadn't quite recovered from his initial bout with Button, when the dog had locked onto his leg.

"I'll, er, put him on."

Perching on the side of the bed, she prodded the sleeping dog awake. At the sound of his mistress's voice, he yipped into the phone once or twice before curling back into a ball and leaving Sheryl to finish the conversation. Somehow, she found herself promising to write faithfully and keep the older woman apprised of Button's health and welfare.

Sniffing, Inga provided a list of absolute essentials. "He takes B-12 and vitamin E twice a week. His vet can supply you with the coated tablets. They're easier for him to swallow. And don't forget his heartworm pills."

"How could I forget those?" Sheryl countered with a grimace.

"Make sure you keep his hair out of his eyes to prevent irritation of the lids."

"I will."

"Don't use rubber bands, though! They pull his hair."

"I won't."

"Oh, I canceled his standing appointment at the stud. You'll have to call them back and reinstate him."

"Excuse me?"

"Button's descended from a line of champions," Inga explained in a teary, quavering voice so different from the one that had shouted obscenities at Harry and Ev that her listener found it hard to believe she was the same woman. "We could charge outrageous stud fees if we wanted to, you know, but we just go there so my precious can, well, enjoy himself."

Sheryl blinked. She hadn't realized her responsibilities would include pimping for Button. She was still dealing with that mind-boggling revelation when Inga sniffed.

"He's very virile. They always offer me pick of the litter." She paused. "You may keep one of his pups in exchange for taking care of him. Or perhaps two, since you work and a pet shouldn't be left alone all day."

"Th-thank you."

Underwhelmed by the magnanimous offer, Sheryl glanced at the tight black-and-white ball on her bed. She could just imagine Harry's reaction if two or three Buttons crawled under the covers with him in the middle of the night.

Assuming Harry ever got back to Albuquerque to get under the covers.

Sighing, she copied down the last of Inga's instructions, held the phone to the dog's ear a final time and hung up. She stood beside the bed for a moment, staring down into her companion's buggy black eyes.

"What do you say, fella? Wanna share a pizza after I get out of the shower?"

Chapter 15

The glossy postcard leaped out at Sheryl from the sheaf of mail in her hand.

Tahiti.

A pristine stretch of sandy beach. A fringe of deep-green banyan trees. An aquamarine sea laced with white, lapping at the shore.

Resolutely, she fought down the urge to turn the postcard over and peek at the message on the back. She'd had enough vicarious adventures as a result of reading other people's mail to last her a while.

She won the brief struggle, but still couldn't bring herself to shove the card in the waiting post office box. For just a moment, she indulged a private fantasy and imagined herself on that empty stretch of beach with Harry. She saw him splashing toward her in the surf. The sun bronzed his lean, hard body. The breeze off the sea ruffled his dark hair. His gold-flecked eyes gleamed with—

"You okay, Sher?"

"What?" Startled out of the South Pacific, she glanced up guiltily to meet Elise's look. "Yes, I'm fine."

"You're thinking about the marshal again, aren't you? You've got that…that lost look on your face."

Sheryl flashed the postcard at her friend. "I was thinking about Tahiti."

Elise pursed her lips.

"All right, all right. I was thinking about Tahiti and Harry."

Nudging aside a stack of mail, the new mom cleared a space on the table between the banks of postal boxes and hitched a hip on the corner. She'd insisted on coming back to work, declaring that her ex-mother-in-law, her parents, her two boys and her regular baby-sitter were more than enough to care for the newest addition to the Hart family. She still hadn't fully regained the endurance required for postal work, though. Sheryl scooped up her bundle and added it to the stack in her hand.

"How long has it been now since Harry left?" Elise demanded as her friend fired the mail into the appropriate boxes. "A week? Eight days?"

"Nine, but who's counting?"

"You are! I am! Everyone in the post office is."

"Well, you can stop counting. He promised he'd come back. He will."

"Oh, Sher, he said he'd come back after the arraignment last week. Then he had to fly to Miami. I hate for you to…"

Buck Aguilar rumbled by with a full cart, drowning out the rest of her comment. Sheryl didn't need to hear it. The worry in her eyes spoke its own language.

"He'll be back, Elise. He promised."

"I believe you," the other woman grumbled. "I just don't like seeing you jump every time the phone rings, or spending your evenings walking that obnoxious little hair ball."

"Give Button time," Sheryl replied, laughing. "He grows on you."

"Ha! That'll be the day. He almost took off my hand at the wrist when I made the mistake of reaching for the baby before Butty-boo was finished checking him out. Here, give me the last stack. I'll finish it."

"I've got it. You just sit and gather your strength for the hordes waiting in the lobby. We have to open in a few minutes."

Elise swung her sneakered foot, a small frown etched on her brow. Sheryl smiled to herself. Her friend still couldn't quite believe that she would prefer the marshal—or anyone else!—over Brian Mitchell. Despite the long talk the two women had shared, Elise had yet to work through her own feelings of guilt and secret longing.

She would. After watching her and Brian together, Sheryl didn't doubt that they'd soon reach the point she herself had come to this past week. They were meant for each other. Just as she and Harry were.

She'd wait for him. However long it took. Wherever his job sent him. She wasn't her mother, and Harry certainly wasn't her father. They'd wring every particle of happiness out of their time together and look forward to their next reunion with the same delicious anticipation that curled in Sheryl's tummy now.

After zinging the last of the box mail into its slot, she slammed the metal door. "Come on, kiddo. We'd better get our cash drawers from the safe. We've only got…"

She glanced at the clock in the central work space and felt her heart sommersault. Striding through the maze of filled mail carts was a tall, unmistakable figure in tight jeans, a blue cotton shirt and a rumpled linen gray sport coat.

"Harry!"

Sheryl flew toward him, scattering letters and advertising fliers and postcards as she went. He caught her up in his arms and whirled her around. The room had barely stopped spinning before he bent his head and covered her mouth with his. Instantly, the whole room tilted crazily again.

Flinging her arms around his neck, she drank in his kiss. It was better than she remembered. Wild. Hot. Hungry. When he lifted his head, she dragged in great, gulping breaths and let the questions tumble out.

"When did you get in? Why didn't you call? What happened in Miami?"

Grinning, he kissed her again, much to the interest of the various personnel who stopped their work to watch.

"Twenty minutes ago. I didn't want to take the time. And we nailed the arms manufacturer Gunderson was supplying."

"Good!"

Laughing at her fierce exclamation, he hefted her higher in his arms and started for the back door.

"Wait a minute!" Sheryl was more than willing to let him carry her right out of the post office, but she needed to cover her station. "I've got to get someone to take the front counter for me."

"It's all arranged," he told her, his eyes gleaming.

"What is?"

"The postmaster general got a call from the attorney general early this morning, Miss Hancock. You're being recommended for a citation for your part in apprehending an escaped fugitive and suspected killer." The gleam deepened to a wicked glint. "You've also been granted the leave you requested. There's a temp on the way down to fill in for you."

"I seem to be having some trouble recalling the fact that I asked for leave."

"I wouldn't be surprised, with all you've gone through lately." Harry wove his way through the carriers' stations. "You asked for two weeks for your honeymoon."

Sheryl opened her mouth, shut it, opened it again. A thousand questions whirled around in her head. Only one squeaked out.

"Two weeks, huh?"

"Two weeks," he confirmed. "Unless you don't have a current passport, in which case we'll have to tack on a few extra days so we can stop over in Washington to pull some strings."

He slowed, his grin softening to a smile so full of tenderness that Sheryl's throat closed.

"I want to take you to Heidelburg, sweetheart, and stand beside you on the castle ramparts when the Neckar River turns gold in the sunset. I want to watch your face the first time you see the spires of Notre Dame rising out of the morning mists. I want to make love to you in France and Italy and Germany and wherever else we happen to stop for an hour or a day or a night."

"Oh, Harry."

He eased his arm from under her knees. Sheryl's feet slid to the floor, but she didn't feel the black tiles under her sneakers. Not with Harry's hands locked loosely around her waist and his heart thumping steadily against hers.

"I know you said it was too soon for commitments and promises, but I've had a lot of time to think this past week."

"Me, too," she breathed.

"I don't want almost, Sheryl. I want you now and forever."

He brushed back her hair with one hand. All trace of amusement left his eyes.

"The regional director's position here in the Albuquerque office comes open next month. The folks in D.C. tell me the job's mine if I want it."

Her pounding pulse stilled. She wanted Harry, as much as he wanted her. But she wouldn't try to hold him with either tears or a love that strangled.

"Do you want it, Harry?"

"Yes, sweetheart, I do. It'll mean less time on the road, although I can't guarantee I'll have anything resembling regular office hours or we'll enjoy a routine home life."

Sheryl could have told him that she'd learned her lesson with Brian. On her list of top-ten priorities, a comfortable routine now ranked about number twenty-five. All that mattered, all she cared about, was the way his touch made her blood sing, and the crinkly lines at the corners of his eyes, and his soft, silky mustache and...

"I'm a deputy marshal," he said quietly. "The service is in my blood."

"I know."

"So are you. I carried your smile and your sun-streaked hair and your little moans of delight with me day and night for the past week. I love you, Sheryl. I want to live the rest of my life with you, if you'll have me, and take you to all the places you dreamed about."

A sigh drifted on the air behind her. She didn't even glance around. She didn't care how many of her co-workers had gathered to hear Harry's soft declaration. One corner of his mustache tipped up.

"I thought about buying a ring and getting down on one knee and doing the whole romantic bit," he told her ruefully, "but I don't want to waste our time with almost-anythings. I want to go right for the real thing. Right here. Right now."

He would, she thought with a smile.

"There's a judge waiting for us at the federal building," he said gruffly. "He'll do the deed as soon as we get the license."

An indignant sputter sounded just behind Sheryl. Elise protested vehemently. "You have to call your mother, Sher! At least give her time to drive up from Las Cruces!"

"The judge will do the deed as soon as your mother gets here," Harry amended gravely, holding her gaze with his own.

Someone else spoke up. Pat Martinez, Sheryl thought.

"Hey, we want to be there, too! Wait until the shift change this afternoon. We'll shred up all that mail languishing in the dead-letter bin and come down to the courthouse armed with champagne and confetti."

"Champagne and confetti sounds good to me." Harry smiled down at her. "Well?"

"I love you, too," she told him mistily. "I'll have you, Marshal, right here, right now and for the rest of our lives."

Stretching up on her tiptoes, she slid her arms around his neck. He bent his head, and his mouth was only a breath away from hers when she murmured, "There's only one problem. We'll have to take Button with us on this honeymoon. Unless you know someone who will take care of him while we're gone?" she asked hopefully.

"You're kidding, right?"

When she shook her head, he closed his eyes. Sheryl closed her ears to his muttered imprecations. When he opened them again, she saw a look of wry resignation in their golden brown depths.

"All right. We'll pick up a doggie-rat carrier on our way to the airport."

At that moment, she knew she'd never settle for almost-anything again.

* * * * *

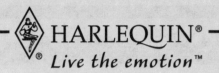

HARLEQUIN®
INTRIGUE®

BREATHTAKING ROMANTIC SUSPENSE

Shared dangers and passions lead to electrifying
romance and heart-stopping suspense!

Every month, you'll meet six new heroes
who are guaranteed to make your spine tingle
and your pulse pound. With them you'll enter
into the exciting world of Harlequin Intrigue—
where your life is on the line
and so is your heart!

THAT'S INTRIGUE—
ROMANTIC SUSPENSE
AT ITS BEST!

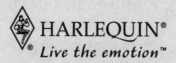

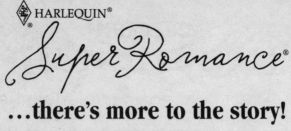
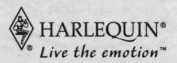

Harlequin® Historical
Historical Romantic Adventure!

*Imagine a time of chivalrous
knights and unconventional ladies,
roguish rakes and impetuous
heiresses, rugged cowboys
and spirited frontierswomen—
these rich and vivid tales will
capture your imagination!*

*Harlequin Historical…
they're too good to miss!*

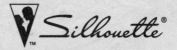

SPECIAL EDITION™

Emotional, compelling stories that capture the intensity of living, loving and creating a family in today's world.

Modern, passionate reads that are powerful and provocative.

nocturne

Dramatic and sensual tales of paranormal romance.

Romances that are sparked by danger and fueled by passion.